CATCH A
FALLEN
ANGEL

Also by Paul Engleman

DEAD IN CENTER FIELD

PAUL ENGLEMAN
CATCH A FALLEN ANGEL

THE MYSTERIOUS PRESS • New York

The characters in this book are fictional. Any inference of similarity to actual living persons is the result of wishful thinking or paranoia on the part of the reader.

The Mysterious Press, 129 West 56th Street, New York, N.Y. 10019

Printed in the United States of America

10 9 8 7 6 5 4 3 2

Library of Congress Cataloging-in-Publication Data

Engleman, Paul.
  Catch a fallen angel.

  I. Title.
PS3555.N426C38   1986   813'.54   86-47547
ISBN 0-89296-174-6 (U.S.A.) (pbk)

This is for Mike and Jo Ann over here, Piero and Giorgio over there.

For all their help, thanks to: my brother Mark, Barb Carney, Paul Gregor, Tony Judge, Anne Mollo-Christensen, Bob Randisi, John Rezek and Tom Young.

CHAPTER 1

It was September 1969. I didn't know the exact date, because I had spilled a can of beer on my desk calendar the night before, effectively wiping out the entire fall.

It wasn't a major loss. I had only been using the calendar to keep track of when bills were due. I hadn't been paying my bills lately, because I was a little short of cash. Looking at the calendar just got me depressed. Maybe that's why I doused it with beer.

Too bad it was my last one.

I was reclining on the couch in my living room, which doubles as my office, trying to figure some things out. I'm thirty-eight years old, and I'm a private investigator. I make my living figuring things out for people. But lately I'd been having some trouble.

For about a month I'd been trying to figure out how three guys had gotten to the moon. Me, I had trouble getting to Times Square from Forty-Second street. Even accepting that they got there, I couldn't figure out how I was able to watch the whole thing on my TV set. I could barely pick up the Yankees, and they played right up in the Bronx.

Things just weren't making sense to me these days.

Richard Nixon was the president of the United States. There was reason to suspect that he had been born on the moon. His opponent in last year's election was a man named Hubert Humphrey. And just last month, one of our other leading

1

politicians, Ted Kennedy, had managed to drive his car off a bridge—with a young woman in it.

Then there was baseball. The Yankees were rotting in the cellar, a disgrace to the pinstripe tradition. Even the Mets were better, and they had a person named Ron Swoboda in their starting lineup. And the Chicago Cubs, for years the doormat of the National League, were closing in on the pennant. To a discerning baseball fan like me, this was very disturbing stuff.

But probably the thing that baffled me most was an event that took place a few weeks before. Half a million kids from all over the country had descended on a farm in upstate New York to see a rock concert. For three days they'd sat out in the rain, listening to raucous music and burning out their brains on drugs and cheap wine. When I was younger we had the Friday night fish fry. Kids nowadays were having Friday night brain fries. They didn't bathe, they were sharing something like twenty-five porta-johns, you couldn't tell the guys from the girls. Worse yet, they were fucking like a school of guppies.

I was mulling over the image of half a million half-naked, brain-fried longhairs boffing each other on a big muddy hill when I finally figured out what it was I was trying to figure out.

These kids were getting laid and I wasn't. I wasn't getting laid and I wasn't getting paid.

It's not like I consider myself some kind of Don Juan. Just that despite my receding hairline, I'm not a bad-looking guy. My second ex-wife even said so the week before when she stopped by to see if I'd forgotten to send her alimony check. I'm not without flaws, I know. But I'm fairly smart, I've got a good sense of humor, I'm told I can be charming at times, I've got excellent table manners, and I'm pretty well-read for a guy who didn't finish college.

But I hadn't gotten laid for three months. This is the kind of thing you worry about when you're thirty-eight and business is slow.

I mixed another gin and tonic in the hope of gaining some insight into the problem. I got as far as the ice cubes and gin when the phone rang. There were three likely possibilities for who was calling. I thought them over while adding the tonic and cutting a wedge of lime.

It could be a collections agent—probably that John Jones again; it could be my second ex-wife informing me that the check (surprise!) had bounced; or it could be my best friend and sometimes partner, Nate Moore, calling to say he hadn't been able to round up a date for me that evening.

We were up to six rings by the time I got to my desk. I deliberated over a sip of my drink. The caller was persistent. You never know when you might get some good news. Positive attitude, right?

I picked up the phone and mumbled the most neutral hello I could muster. One thing I've learned in my business: Never answer your phone by name.

I was glad I hadn't. The person on the other end identified himself as Bill Walters. That was a collections agent moniker if I've ever heard one.

I was wrong. It happens sometimes. I don't like to be wrong, but it has its moments. This turned out to be one of them.

"I'm calling from Chicago," Bill Walters said. "I'm the public relations director for *Paradise* magazine."

"Did I win a contest?"

The voice called Bill Walters had a good chuckle at that. "Oh, no. Is this Mr. Renzler?"

"Yeah," I answered. "You've got the right guy."

"Oh, I was a bit puzzled." He wasn't the only one, but I tried not to let on. "It took so long for you to answer. I thought maybe my secretary had dialed the wrong number."

"Her dialing's impeccable. I was just giving a little dictation to *my* secretary. She's a good dialer, too. But her shorthand leaves a little to be desired."

Walters chuckled again. The guy was an easy laugh. I wouldn't have to waste any of my "A" material on him.

"We thought the secretary in my outer office would answer the phone," I explained. "She must be busy with a client."

"Oh, I hope you're not *too* busy," Walters said. "I was hoping to get you involved in something right away. It's an urgent situation. An emergency that requires immediate attention."

"No, no. You can never be too busy," I said. I always say. "What's the nature of this emergency?"

"I don't think I should divulge any of the details over the phone, but I can tell you that it concerns our upcoming Angel of the Year. Are you familiar with our magazine?"

"Of course I am. I see it regularly." Actually, my subscription had lapsed a few years back. But I had seen one of the *Paradise* centerfolds on "The Joe Franklin Show" the previous week. She was about half my age and had about twice my energy. But I wouldn't have minded trying to swim a few laps with her.

"Can you come to Chicago right away? Mr. Long would like to see you this afternoon."

"Arnold Long wants to see me?"

"Yes, you know of him, I assume."

"Of course." That was no lie. No one in America didn't know Arnold Long, the publisher of *Paradise* magazine and owner of a chain of restaurants called Paradise Rooms. Along with Hugh Hefner and Howard Hughes, Long was one of the best-known entrepreneurial success stories of the twentieth century.

"I'm not sure I can get out there today," I said. "I've got to wrap up a few matters, get a plane—"

"Oh, no. Don't worry about a plane. I'm sending ours to pick you up. The *Paradise 666.*"

"You're sending *that* to New York to get me?" I make a point of trying to sound undaunted, but this was a definite surprise. With the possible exception of Hefner's *Big Bunny* jet, the *Paradise 666* was reputed to be the world's highest-flying round-the-clock orgy. I was a little disturbed that it wasn't being put to better use at the moment.

"No problem. I'll have a limo pick you up at your office and take you to Teterboro Airport in New Jersey. I can have it there in an hour and a half. Is that all right?"

"Sure, fine. But if you wouldn't mind, I'd like to bring along my associate, Nate Moore." Nate was a strong, strapping son of a bitch who worked with me in his spare time. His full-time occupation was painting—canvasses, not houses—but to see him, you would have guessed he was a linebacker for the New York Giants. I met him in 1957 when I was investigating an art theft. Nate's had been one of the paintings stolen from a gallery in the Village. He was a big help when we finally caught up with the three guys who had lifted the stuff. I couldn't have taken them all on alone. With Nate there, I got to stand by and smoke a cigarette.

"No problem," Walters said. "If you're sure he can be ready."

"He'll be ready," I said. A flight on *Paradise 666* wasn't the sort of invitation Nate would pass up. He would've killed me if I didn't take him.

I thought about putting in a few more requests, but I didn't want to press my luck. I did have one more question, though.

"Just out of curiosity, Mr. Walters, did you check my references?"

"Oh yes, they're excellent."

This guy didn't know anyone who knew me very well. Until I met Arnold Long, I was satisfied to leave it at that.

CHAPTER 2

Three hours later, we were landing at Meigs Field, a small airport on the lake—Michigan, I think it is—near downtown Chicago, which locals call the Loop.

If the truth be told, I was a bit disappointed in the *Paradise 666*. From the outside, it looked just like the pictures I had seen—glossy silver emblazoned with the Paradise logo, a bright red apple with a winking black serpent wrapped around it. Inside there were no orgies in progress that I could see, though there were a half dozen blondes on hand to ensure a beautiful flight.

The women were clad in silver go-go boots and white jumpsuits that were so tight they could take your breath away—and probably theirs, too, if they hadn't been unzipped so far. Over their right breasts they wore Paradise logo name badges that could draw blood with one wrong move. Two of the girls appeared to me to be under the age of consent; the other four looked as if they had maybe consented too often.

It was instantly clear that the Angel Flies, as they were called, were on hand to fulfill our every desire—within limits. The limits were basically pouring and repouring drinks, buckling and unbuckling seat belts, adjusting pillows and holding our cues during the billiards tournament. This was not a real tournament; merely a best of five series of eight ball between Nate and me that I won in three straight games. He was shooting with such truculence that at least one ball seemed to hurdle the table on each shot. I thought it might be the altitude, but he later alibied that he enjoyed watching Angel Fly Bonni bending over to retrieve the strays.

Bonni was the youngest of the group. She claimed to be nineteen, but I would have guessed sixteen. By the time you hit your late thirties, you just goddamn can't tell anymore. The oldest was Terri, the Angel Fly Queen, who must have been pushing forty-five. She looked like a fading flower beside the others, but unless you can die of suntan or stretch marks, she still had a few good years left. She also had a nice personality, which has always counted for a lot in my book, especially when it's empty.

At the airport, two more blondes escorted us to a limo and drove us north on Lake Shore Drive to Arnold Long's estate on Lincoln Park West. I don't know if the car had a special name, but it was silver and had the Paradise seal on each door. The girls had names, Mindi and Marla, but no badges. They wore modified versions of the Angel Fly suits, looser but still fetching.

When we arrived, Mindi went to fetch the PR director, Bill Walters, while Marla waited with Nate and me in the foyer. Like mine, Arnold Long's home doubled as his office. The similarity in our operations ended there. The foyer alone was twice the size of my office, bathroom and kitchen included. Where my staff consisted of an ersatz recording of a secretary that Nate had wired for me, Long had two very authentic secretaries stationed at an enormous reception desk that was shaped like—I kid you not—a fig leaf. And while my headquarters were merely called 118 West Seventy-Second Street, Long's place had a glamorous appellative: The Garden of Eden, or simply Eden to those in the know.

Mindi returned with Walters in five minutes. I had expected a runt based on my previous encounters with PR types, but he was what you'd call normal size—about five feet ten inches, 170 pounds. He offered a fish on the shake, however, and that's always a bad sign.

After exchanging pleasantries for a few moments, we got the good news that Mindi and Marla would be accompanying us to our meeting with Arnold Long. Before that, we had to meet Arnie

Long, Arnold's only son and apparent heir to the Paradise throne when Arnold Sr. decided it was time to retire from the grueling regimen of having gorgeous women wait on him all day.

Arnie, I figured from initial observation, had spent too many years being told he was a chip off the old block. He had been to Wharton Business School by way of Princeton, he managed to let us know, but I noticed right off that he hadn't graduated from the Old Spice school of after shave. He was my height, six feet two inches, about ten pounds heavier than my 190 and barely thirty years old. His tone was Ivy League cordial, and he kept us just long enough for the biographical thumb sketch before taking us down the long winding hallways of Eden to the Sanctuary, a room where his dad, Arnold Long, founder and publisher of *Paradise* magazine, spent most of his waking hours.

The Sanctuary was as long as a hockey rink and wider than a football field. At the far end was a swimming pool. It wasn't Olympic size, but you could probably get tired after doing a few laps in it. It was bordered with plastic grass and a dozen lounge chairs. From there it was only a few steps to one of four bars in the room. They were stocked with enough booze to get New York drunk every night until New Year's. Coming toward the near end, there were two Ping-Pong tables and a bank of pinball machines. You like to bowl? There were three lanes. Golf? There was a putting green. Shoot pool? There were four tables. Checkers, chess, backgammon? Pull up a chair at one of the tables.

Nate and I exchanged glances. His eyes were bulging, and I figured mine were doing the same. We were standing in the middle of an adolescent boy's idea of heaven. It was the ultimate tree house. I would have spent the night there gladly. And by the way, Mom and Dad, don't bother coming out to check on me at midnight.

But the Sanctuary was not just a playroom. If the size of a man's desk has any relation to the value of his work, Arnold Long indisputably had the most important job in the world. Of course, he might be scored down a few points for having a desk shaped like a fig leaf. It was the senior version of the one I had marveled at in the reception area.

Arnold Long was not at his desk when we entered. He was lying facedown on one of six leather-matted surgical tables in the center of the room. He was naked, except for a towel that lay across his buttocks. His back was being massaged and pounded by a pair of buxom blondes—one for each end of the towel, I figured.

"Which one of you is Renzler?" His voice was muffled against the leather mat.

I admitted my guilt and walked the twenty steps to his outstretched hand. "No need to get up," I said.

"Don't worry, I won't," he replied.

Nate followed me to the table and winked at Long's attendants while Arnie made formal introductions. Bill Walters was stationed nearby to correct him if he made any mistakes. He didn't.

Arnie's father barely looked at us, but his shake was sturdy. "I'd offer you gentlemen a sauna before we start the meeting, but I've got an important party in a couple of hours," he said.

I told him I understood, but of course I didn't.

"You're both welcome to attend." Long angled slightly to make eye contact with us.

I shrugged. "That's OK. We wouldn't want to get in the way at an important party." The reply earned me a speak-for-yourself elbow in the ribs from Nate.

"I mean you're *expected* to attend." Arnold's voice was forceful but cordial. "You're my guests, and my guests attend my parties. It's as simple as that." He turned over suddenly and sat up. With perfect timing, one of the blondes adjusted the towel to prevent our glimpsing Arnold Long's genitalia. I was glad there were two of them.

"Mindi and Marla will give you rubdowns," Long said, motioning for us to take the two tables on either side of him. "Walters will fix you a drink."

With Mindi's assistance, Nate was naked and on the table in no time. Marla was having a little more trouble with me. Very possibly because I wasn't being as cooperative as my associate.

My reticence did not go unnoticed by the Bard of Paradise, as he was sometimes referred to in his magazine. "Have you got a body thing, Renzler?"

"A body thing?"

"A hangup. Arnie, tell Renzler my philosophy about body hangups."

"Dad believes the human body is beautiful," Arnie explained. I watched for embarrassment in his face but couldn't find any. "Dad thinks too many people in our culture feel self-conscious about their bodies. Dad isn't self-conscious at all."

I shot a quick glance at Arnold Long and thought maybe he should be. It was hard to estimate his size while he was sitting down, but he couldn't have been taller than five feet eight inches. There was enough mass on him to fill a six-foot frame quite adequately, no doubt a result of regular indulgence in Paradise Room prime rib.

"I see," I answered. "I've never really thought about it that much, but I'm inclined to think there comes a time in every man's life when he shouldn't be seen naked by anyone other than his lover, his doctor or his cat. I guess I am a bit self-conscious about my battle scars. Knife and bullet wounds are pretty unsightly."

"They don't bother me," Marla said. I was on the table now, and she was pressing her long, slender fingers into my back. Damn, it did feel good.

"Me either," Arnold Long said. "The human body is beautiful. Of course, some are nicer than others, but there's nothing for you to be ashamed of, Renzler. After a day or two at Eden, your hangup will be gone."

"It may take him a week, Mr. Long," Nate piped up from his mat. Mindi was working him over pretty good, and he was breathing heavily—too heavily, as far as I was concerned.

I tried to shoot him a look that killed, but I was at a bad angle. I'm blind in my left eye, another occupational casualty. This one I suffered in my previous career, when I played AA baseball for the Richmond Sailors. I was hit by a wild pitch thrown by a wild pitcher whose first name was Manuel and whose last name I could never pronounce. I later heard that he pitched for the Pittsburgh Pirates, but he didn't last long. Control problems, you know. He outlasted me, though. My career ended in Richmond.

Bill Walters returned with our drinks and a cigar for Arnold Long. One of Long's towel blondes lit it for him, and he began to speak. I sipped my bourbon and tried not to let Marla's fingernails interfere with my concentration.

It was no easy task, but I'm a professional.

CHAPTER 3

"**I**'ll try to make this brief," Arnold Long began.

Ordinarily, that opening is a sure sign that a verbal assault of unmitigated boredom is imminent, but this time I didn't mind. I had a big drink and a date with a hand other than my own. Plus I was very interested in hearing about the Paradise legend from the man who started it all.

"I don't think I'm being presumptuous in assuming that you're familiar with the Paradise Corporation. Our logo is one of the most widely recognized symbols in the world, possibly in the whole universe."

Nate and I understood that this was the correct time to chuckle, and we did. Arnie and Walters had their cheeks creased a full five seconds before Arnold Long reached the punch line. They were seated side by side on the table next to Arnold's. The girls by contrast did not laugh at all. I had a feeling they weren't supposed to be listening.

"I started this business ten years ago with 666 dollars to my name. I started it the year of Sputnik. Now our country has put a man on the moon. That's significant of something, I think. The company has grown—well, you know how it's grown. Meteorically, quantum leaps and bounds. Some people call me a genius, others call me lucky. Some think I've had as much influence on the sociosexual development of the United States in the last decade as anyone else in the entire century."

Long paused. "And of course there are those who think I'm the biggest asshole in the world."

"I've heard you called them all," I told him. He seemed pleased. I didn't add that I'd mostly heard him called the last.

"Well, yes. I merely like to say that I feel I've done rather well for a boy named Arnold."

This was another designated laugh spot. The men laughed.

"Now I assume you see my magazine every so often."

"Every month," Nate said. He had turned over on his back, and his breathing was regular again. I was relieved. Body hangup philosophy notwithstanding, I was sure Arnold Long wouldn't have been too pleased if Nate dropped anchor all over one of his rubdown tables.

"OK, that's good," Arnold said. "Then you know that each month we have a girl in our centerfold, our Angel of the Month."

"Right," Nate said. "Then at the end of the year, the readers vote for their favorite girl, and whoever gets the most votes is named Angel of the Year. That's in the March issue, right?"

The guffaws were soft at first. But after a moment, Marla, Mindi and the towel girls had joined in. When Arnold Long finally sat up after being doubled over, he smiled at Nate and said, "Walters, why don't you explain."

"Mr. Moore," the PR director said, "you'll be learning quite a bit about the affairs of the Paradise Corporation over the next few days. I do hope you'll bear in mind at all times that these matters are of the highest confidence. At certain times, it's necessary—"

"Oh, hell, I'll tell him." Arnold was puffing hard on his cigar. It didn't smell half bad, though I've never been a cigar man. "What Walters is trying to tell you is that the readers' votes don't count. We don't bother to count 'em. We don't have time to count 'em. We're too busy enjoying ourselves to count 'em!"

"You don't count the votes." Nate's voice was tentative but not incredulous.

"No, we don't. There's only one vote."

"Let me guess," Nate said.

That got a laugh, from staff and distaff alike. But Arnold became serious a moment later.

"What Walters says is correct, though, gentleman. You are becoming privy to matters of the highest confidence. You must speak to no one about them. I must have it that way."

"You will," I assured him. "That comes with our services. Talking to us is like talking to a pair of priests."

I thought Arnold Long recoiled slightly at the clerical analogy, which was fine by me. I like to like my clients, but I don't like them telling me what I can and can't do. Even if my references are lousy these days.

"Fine, that's settled." Arnold looked at his watch and his tone became businesslike. "Let me give you some background. We've always had problems with the media. Many of them resent my success, others think we encourage immorality. In two weeks, we will have another competitor on the newsstand, a magazine thrown together by a scurrilous man named Len Wyder. Knowing Wyder, I'm certain it will be done in the worst possible taste. For years I've tried to publish a quality publication, one that is at all times sophisticated and tasteful. When Wyder's magazine comes out, it will no doubt cause some controversy. And you can be sure that *Paradise* will suffer guilt by association. We can put a man on the moon, but in terms of its attitude toward sexuality, this country is in the Dark Ages."

I didn't know where Long was going, but I nodded when he paused and looked at me. I was sitting up now. "What's the name of Wyder's magazine?" I asked.

"*Nook*, N-O-O-K."

"Very subtle," I said. "And the centerfold will be called . . ."

"That's right. Nookie." Long shook his head.

"You don't think he'll be able to compete with you?"

Arnold let out a snort that was echoed by his son and Walters. "I'm not the least bit threatened, Renzler. The competitors are all over the place. First there was *Playboy*, or even *Esquire*, if you want to count that. Then I came along. Now a man named Guccione in New York is starting a magazine called *Penthouse*. I've held my own and I'll always hold my own. I give Wyder six months, a year at most, until his rag folds. But in the meantime, we will have to endure another assault from the prudes and the moralists and the censors. I've been through that before. I still get hate mail here. I get death threats."

Long fell silent. He seemed to be leading up to something but was unsure of how to get there.

"Is that the reason you called me? Because of Wyder?"

"No, as I said, that's background. What I called you about is a matter of much greater gravity. And, as I also said before, *absolute secrecy.*"

Long looked to Nate and me for acknowledgment. We nodded.

"Gentlemen, our Angel of the Year is missing."

"Missing?"

"That's right, Mr. Moore. Missing. She is our October Angel of the Month. That issue comes out September twenty-first. Is that correct, Arnie?"

"The twenty-second, Dad."

"Close enough. Her name is Sherri West. She is scheduled to go on a publicity tour for us in Minneapolis on that day. After that, we will shoot her for the Angel of the Year issue, next March."

"How long has she been gone?" I asked.

"Ten days now. We all—Bill, Arnie, the photographer and I— thought she went to St. Louis to see her parents. When Sherri left, she said she wanted some time to herself. She's a very independent girl. She was supposed to stay in touch with the photographer, Steve Farrell. But Steve, I learned yesterday, has not seen or heard from her since we have. I had Walters check up on her yesterday. Tell them what you learned, Walters."

"You see, Sherri's mother and father are not entirely pleased with her association with Paradise. I didn't want to alarm them, so I checked on her plane reservations. Sherri never went to St. Louis."

"Not by plane," I said. "Could she have driven or taken the train?"

"I thought of that. So I called her parents anonymously. Her father said she was in Chicago. He said she hadn't been home since last Christmas."

"Have you checked anywhere else? Have you talked to her friends or other relatives?"

Walters nodded. "It looks like she's vanished."

"What do you think?" Arnold Long asked. "That's not good, is it?"

"It's never good when someone disappears," I said. "There are a million things that can happen. When it's a beautiful girl you're talking about, there are a million and a half."

"I was afraid you'd say something like that. I must find Sherri."

The finality of Long's tone gave way to a dead silence. "I assume you have a picture of her," Nate said. His humor was lost on all but me.

"Of course. Walters will give you one."

"We'll need more than that," I said. "You probably have some suspicions, if you think about it. Is there someone who might want to get at Sherri? Someone who might want to get at *you* through Sherri?"

"Mr. Renzler, I've made a lot of enemies in a very short period of time. There are crazies out there. Hate groups. Girls who desperately wanted to be centerfolds but didn't have what it takes. I couldn't begin to make a list."

"I'm afraid you might have to try."

"There are some angles for you to explore. Arnie and Walters are familiar with the situation. They'll supply you with any information you might need." Long got down from his table, assisted by the towel blondes. "Well," he said, "it's time for my bath."

Marla secured my towel with professional ease as I returned to my feet. Long extended his hand.

"Whatever your fee is, I'll double it, Renzler. You and Moore may stay here at Eden for as long as you like. If you need to travel out of town, my plane is at your disposal. I've never felt the need for a large security staff around here, but maybe I've been wrong. After you find Sherri, there could be a permanent position here for you as security director. Herman Winkles says you're the best detective in the business. I hope he's right."

So that's how Long got my name. I used to ask, but these days I felt lucky just to get the business. Herman Winkles was one of New York's biggest real estate developers. He was also one of the world's biggest pains in the ass. He had hired me the year before to find his teenage daughter. I did—at the Krishna temple in Brooklyn.

Long still held my hand. "You must find Sherri."

"We'll do our best, Mr. Long. But . . ."

"But what?"

"Ten days may not seem like a long time, but it is. You have to consider the possibility that Sherri West could be dead."

Arnold Long shook his head. "I don't believe that, Renzler. My instincts tell me that Sherri is still alive. My instincts are what made me the man I am today. Find her."

My instincts told me that something more than instincts were making Long so certain Sherri West was alive. Something like not telling me everything he knew.

But I didn't bother to press him. I could get it out of Arnie.

CHAPTER 4

Arnold Long strolled out of the Sanctuary accompanied by his towel blondes and followed by his son and PR director. Marla and Mindi gave Nate and me a good dressing-up, then walked us down the winding halls to a conference room where Walters and Arnie were waiting. Though it was a posh room, equipped with a bar, the conference room was more conducive to conferring than the Sanctuary. The ladies served us another round of drinks but left right away. They promised to meet us at the reception desk when we were finished, then escort us to the party.

To a guy who hadn't been on a date for a month, this sounded like an excellent plan.

Bill Walters busied himself setting up a slide projector while Arnie Long ran through the confidentiality speech again. It was brief, so I didn't bother with any more ecclesiastic analogies. Walters pressed some buttons on one wall, the lights dimmed, and a projection screen lowered from the ceiling.

The first slide that came on the screen was a photo of a white male, about thirty years old. He wasn't exactly unwashed, but his grooming left a little to be desired.

"That's Paul Johnson," Arnie Long said. "His friends call him Pablo. I regret to say that Sherri seems to be one of his friends. Johnson is, for all intents and purposes, a loser. I don't know how Sherri came to know him, but she had been spending a considerable amount of time with him. Dad especially did not like Johnson. He thought he was a bad influence on Sherri."

"How so?" Nate asked.

"He fancies himself a revolutionary. Whenever he came around, he was always talking about some protest march or demonstration. He was abrasive, obnoxious. He had a habit of lecturing people about antimaterialism. I believe he takes a lot of drugs.

"Dad thought he was a hypocrite. My father is a very generous man, but does not tolerate a person who drinks his liquor and takes advantage of his hospitality and then accuses people of being bourgeois."

"I can't blame him for that," I said. "Johnson sounds like a peculiar character for Sherri to be hanging around with. Of course, I don't know her personally, but I've seen a few of your centerfolds on TV and none of them seems very concerned about the progress of the revolution. Was Sherri into drugs?"

"Yes, I'm inclined to think she was," Arnie said. "She sometimes seemed distracted, kind of aloof. Some of our other girls have become involved in drugs. She acted like them."

"Have you checked out Johnson since Sherri left?" Nate asked.

"We've tried. But no luck. No one knows where he lives. Walters made some inquiries. Tell them, Walters."

"He worked at some sort of radical bookstore. Or at least that's where he said he worked. Every time Sherri brought him around, he had one of those leftist newspapers or pamphlets with him. He used to leave them around here for people to read. We'd just throw the crap out."

"Where's the bookstore?"

"On Addison, up the block from Wrigley Field. I think it's called People's Books."

"That sounds about right," I said. "Did you go up there?"

"I called, but I couldn't even find out if he worked there," Walters said. "The guy who answered the phone called me a capitalist pig. He asked if I was working for the CIA."

"Did your father ever talk to Johnson? You said he thought he was a hypocrite." It was dark in the room, but I could see Arnie and Walters checking with each other before Arnie answered my question.

"Very little. Dad can be rather preemptory, if you know what I mean. He asked Johnson to leave Eden and never return."

"I don't imagine Sherri much appreciated that," Nate said.

"She didn't seem to mind that I noticed," Arnie said.

"That seems surprising, if Johnson was her boyfriend," Nate said.

"No, that's the strange aspect of their relationship. It was platonic. He insisted upon it. He seemed to think that he had transcended sexuality. He was almost moralistic. Johnson pretty much ridiculed the entire Paradise concept. All the while drinking my father's liquor and lecturing Sherri about socialism."

"Sounds like a nutcase or a drug burnout," Nate said.

Or both. And a bore, as well. But I was beginning to see how Sherri West might be attracted to someone like Johnson. To a girl of twenty with a limited intellect, he might have seemed like a refreshing contrast to the Paradise concept, as Arnie Long called it.

"The guy was pretty bad news," Walters said.

"Did anyone that you know of point this out to Sherri?" I asked.

"Well, I didn't exactly think it was my place to do so," Arnie replied.

"What about your father?"

Arnie and Walters were exchanging looks again. "Well, I guess he did," Arnie answered. "They had an argument of sorts a while back."

"Of sorts? About Johnson?"

Arnie paused. "Probably."

"How long ago?"

"Well, I'm not sure exactly. Two weeks ago, perhaps."

"No offense, Arnie, but I think you can do better than that." Nate's always been good with that kind of comment. "Was it eleven days ago, maybe? Like the night before she left?"

Arnie sighed loud and long. "Don't tell Dad I told you this. I promised him I wouldn't. That appears to be the primary reason why Sherri left Eden. Dad was experiencing some guilt for having banished Johnson and upsetting Sherri. So he had us arrange the St. Louis trip. It was his belief that Sherri would take a more mature view of the situation if she spent some time away from Johnson."

"I see. No wonder he seems so certain she's still alive." To Nate, I said, "Looks like all we've got to do is find Johnson."

"That may not be easy," Arnie said. "And there's more, and it's worse."

Oh, yes, the slide projector.

Walters switched to the next slide, a photostat of a hand-printed note on People Against Pornography letterhead. It was addressed to Sherri West:

YOU ARE UNCLEAN. GOD WILL JUDGE AND PUNISH.

Walters put four more letters on the screen. The words varied slightly, but the format and message did not. There was no specific threat of retribution other than divine intervention.

"We receive these notes with some regularity. But these particular ones are strange," Arnie said.

"Why is that?" Nate asked.

"Well, every month for approximately the past two years, the Angel of the Month has received a note like this. We believe that a reverend here in Chicago is responsible for them. We have not been able to ascertain what the name of his church is. I doubt very seriously whether he even has one. Every so often, he brings a group of his followers to Eden—they all seem to be young boys, teenagers—and they march outside for an hour or so with signs. They demonstrate outside the Playboy Building, too. The strange aspect of these letters is that they usually don't arrive until the magazine is on the newsstand. There is usually one, occasionally two. Sherri began getting her notes about a month ago. They were coming almost every day."

"What's the name of this reverend?" I asked.

"Oh, yes. Whitey Howard."

"Whitey?" Nate was shaking his head in disbelief.

"That's what I'm told."

"Do you have any of the other notes?" I asked Walters. "The *un*strange ones?"

He did, and he flashed it up on the screen.

"It's uppercase, lowercase," Nate observed. "The others are all capital letters."

"The handwriting might even be different," I added.

"Are you guys saying that the letters were done by different people?" Walters asked.

"It's possible," I answered, thinking it was closer to probable. But I figured it would be wiser to check out Reverend Whitey before we began raising questions about an inside job. There seemed to be enough trouble in Paradise, already. "We'll have to see a few more notes."

"I have some in the files," Walters said.

"How did Sherri feel about the notes?" I asked. "Did they upset her?"

"I was traveling on business a lot last month. Walters knows a lot more about that."

"She wasn't all that bothered at first," the PR man said. "Reverend Whitey's letters are kind of a joke around here. We've never taken them very seriously. A couple of the girls even got upset when they didn't get one. But I guess it was around the second week of August when Arnie was away that Sherri did get kind of frightened. One night she went back to her apartment, and she thought a guy was following her. When she got up the next morning, she found a letter under her door. That one definitely shook her, which I can certainly understand."

"I had the impression Sherri was living here," I said.

"Yes, she does live here, at least most of the time. But she has an apartment, and every so often, she'd go home. Maybe Mr. Long was having an important party that night. After she got that letter at home, she stayed here every night."

"Until ten days ago," Nate added.

"Yes," Walters said. "That's what I meant."

"Have you checked for Sherri at her apartment?" I asked.

"Yes, we did," Arnie said. "Walters went over there personally yesterday after Dad talked to Steve Farrell. The engineer let him in, but it appeared she hasn't been home."

"What about Farrell? He's the photographer, right?"

"I'm afraid he won't be of much help to you," Arnie said. "Steve is arguably the best in the business, but he's not exactly playing with a full deck. Too many drugs. He's taken a lot of LSD. Don't mention that to my father, incidentally. He's fond of Steve. He believes people should be permitted to do as they wish, since that is the Paradise concept. But Dad has never understood why people take drugs. Especially LSD."

"Were Sherri and Steve Farrell close?" I asked.

"Yes, I'm sure they were." Arnie was rubbing his eyes. Walters had turned on the lights again. "Photographers and the girls they photograph usually have a special kind of relationship."

"How special was theirs?" Nate asked my question for me.

"Do you mean, were they fucking?"

"Yeah, that's what I mean."

"I suppose they might have been. They had a certain rapport. But I can't answer for Steve. But I should warn you: Don't be surprised if you get a confused answer. Steve Farrell seems to get more strung out each time I talk to him."

"Is there somebody else in town other than Pablo that Sherri could be staying with?" I asked.

Arnie shook his head, but Walters answered in a tentative voice. "Maybe Cindi."

"She wouldn't stay with her, Bill. They don't even talk to each other anymore."

"Who's that?"

"Her sister."

"Why don't they talk to each other?"

"It's a mystery to me," Arnie answered. "I gather they've never liked each other."

I looked at Walters. He didn't look mystified. But he didn't offer an opinion.

"Do you know how to get in touch with her?" I asked Arnie.

"Oh, sure. She works at the Paradise Room. It's on Clark Street. I think you'd be wasting your time talking to her. I already have. She hasn't spoken to Sherri in six months."

Arnie got up from the table. "I think that pretty much wraps things up. I have to get ready for the party myself. Bill will get you all the information you need—addresses and photos and such."

I finished off my drink. "Just one more question, Arnie. Your father is obviously very concerned about finding Sherri. But I get the impression it goes a lot deeper than professional concern."

Arnie seemed to bristle, even though the question was just begging to be asked.

Nate tried to lighten things up a bit in his own heavy-handed way. "What my partner is trying to say is, were they fucking?"

Arnie was not amused. "My father is a very unique man. He has sexual relationships with many of the Angels. We are very open about sex around here. Sexual freedom is the cornerstone of the Paradise ideology. But along with that comes the absence of jealousy or possessiveness. My father does not have those kind of hangups."

"I wasn't thinking about your father's problems," I explained. "I was thinking about Sherri's." My volume was normal, but my tone was sharp. "She's twenty years old. She hasn't been living in Eden for the last ten years. In a few weeks, nude pictures of her are going to be on view for a few million men to see. She's been getting crank letters. She's had some loser telling her sex is bad and revolution is good. She's been living in a place where sex is everything. It's no wonder she needed some time alone. I imagine she was pretty confused. I also imagine she had some hangups. Many of us do, you know."

I had a feeling Arnie Long wasn't accustomed to being called on a point of his father's theology. He sat in silence for a moment, then stood up, smiling.

"I don't have any hangups," he said. "I just hope we hired the right people for this job."

Walters started grinning as soon as Arnie left the room. The PR director had been cringing throughout my sermon. "Boy, oh boy," he said. "You really gave it to him."

"You know," Nate said, "I've got a feeling young Arnie don't get laid as much as he might like people to believe."

Walters shook his head. "If you guys ever think of changing careers," he said, "steer clear of PR."

CHAPTER 5

I have to admit, it was quite a party. Arnold Long's extravaganzas were legendary—mainly because they were written up with splashy photos in *Paradise*—and I wasn't disappointed.

There were drinks galore and a spread of cold cuts that would have led you to believe that Long had invented the smorgasbord. The place looked like it was under siege from an invasion of blondes. There were two of them for every guy, and that ratio doesn't include the ones who were fetching food and pouring booze for Long's guests, most of whom were rubes in town for some sort of business convention.

Most of the girls had on their party dresses, which looked to have been designed at a shop that was running short of material. The ones who didn't wear formal dresses were clad in outfits that were close relatives of the bikini. They were gyrating to acid rock music that was pumped into the Serpent's Room through professionally placed speakers. A few of the girls had occasional problems keeping Mother Nature's gifts under wraps. And though I didn't actually see any being smoked, the smell of marijuana was in evidence.

Nate recognized many of the women from their photo spreads in the magazine. With a little less alcohol in his system, he probably could have identified them by the month and year of their appearance. Lacking in the peculiar set of motor skills that dancing requires, I contented myself with sitting in a corner, sucking down drinks and trying not to feel embarrassed for Nate, who was showing no such restraint.

As an official representative of Paradise, Marla was required to mingle with the guests. But she reserved most of her mingling for me. It was quite pleasant, as well as educational.

In the year that she had worked there, Marla had been a close observer of the activities at Eden, and she was ready and willing to share her observations with me. I learned, for instance, that Sherri West had indeed been Arnold Long's number one girl for the last six months. But Sherri eventually came to resent the attention Long's other ladies lavished upon him. They argued loud and often. According to Marla, Arnold was given to long lectures on the pettiness of jealousy, but he had exploded when Sherri started inviting Pablo Johnson to Eden. Sherri did not especially like Johnson, Marla thought, but she kept him around to annoy Arnold Long.

Then there was the matter of Sherri's older sister, Cindi, who worked as a Cherub at the Paradise Room. Arnie Long met Cindi at a Chicago bar, and it was sex at first sight. Soon afterward, his father's hormones began to spin. Cindi was photographed for an Angel of the Month spread, and Arnold was thought to be considering her for Angel of the Year. But Cindi made the mistake of bringing Sherri into the big picture, and from then on, there was trouble in Paradise.

Arnold Long quickly became predisposed toward Sherri, and plans for Cindi's photo spread were soon disposed of. When Cindi wasn't fighting with Arnold, she was fighting the booze and losing. She began to eat like a horse and soon after that began to look like one. After a few embarrassing episodes of public neighing, she was put out to graze at the Paradise Room.

Cindi West's photos never ran in the magazine.

Raucous music notwithstanding, I could have sat there talking with Marla a lot longer. But she was tired and wanted to leave. She said Arnold Long's parties were becoming something of a drain on her. I could see why. They looked like more fun for the men than for the women.

There were two other questions I wanted to ask Marla, and they had nothing to do with the investigation. Despite my experience over the years, I didn't have the nerve to ask the second. So I asked the first.

"How is it that you came to work here?"

She threw back her head and laughed. I could see her blue eyes sparkling. Well, I guess it was hard to see them in the dim light, but in the glow of the booze I enjoyed thinking they were sparkling.

"It was a sociology project," she said.

Now it was my turn to laugh.

"I'm serious. I thought it would make a good research paper."

"I see." I'm sure my expression was skeptical. "What grade are you in?"

"I'm in college, wise guy. But I took a leave of absence after I got the job. The pay is good here." Her eyes *were* sparkling this time. "And . . . I like sex."

Oh, boy. That sounded like the answer to my second question.

I'm sorry to report that it wasn't. When we got to the door to her room, she gave me a rain check instead of an invitation.

"I like you, Renzler," she said. She was kissing my neck with a thoroughness I'm not accustomed to. "You're a nice guy. A lot nicer than most of the other guys who hang around here."

From what I had seen of the guests at the party, I didn't think it was much of a compliment. But I didn't complain.

"I just don't feel like balling you tonight. I'd rather wait till tomorrow, when we know each other a little better. Is that OK?"

I'd be lying if I said I wasn't disappointed. But after three months of involuntary celibacy, I figured it wouldn't hurt to wait another twenty-four hours. Unless I wound up getting shot the next day, in which case it would probably be a better idea to get a good night's sleep.

"Sure, fine," I said, a little startled by her bluntness. I leaned in for another kiss, but she plugged me with a wet one on the forehead. It was going to take me a few more swings to get my timing back.

By the time I got back to the Serpent's Room, the party was winding down. The girls were all looking a little the worse for wear, and most of them had chosen wall-leaning as an alternative to gyrating. The music was country mellow now, and what few conventioneers were left had taken to slumping in their chairs. Arnold Long was no longer in evidence. Arnie and Bill Walters were circulating among the hangers-on, shaking the hands of those who were standing and shaking the shoulders of those who were sitting. Nate and Mindi, it appeared, had departed for more intimate fun.

I returned to my room and reclined on the bed, thinking, but not too hard, about what Marla had said.

A nice guy. I've heard that one before. Leo Durocher, the manager of the Cubs, had it right when he said, "Nice guys finish last." Durocher knew what he was talking about. He had the goddamn Cubs in first place.

But all in all, I didn't feel bad. I was working again—on a plum assignment, at that. Besides, I knew something about myself that Marla didn't.

Sometimes, I'm not such a nice guy.

CHAPTER 6

Early Friday morning I woke up to the sound of someone opening the door to my room. I'm not what you'd call a morning person, but my survival instincts are very sharp, even on a hangover. By the time my visitor got to the foot of the bed, I was sitting up and pointing my gun at her.

"Hi," she said. "I was going to surprise you." Her voice was sheepish. It might have been more sheepish, if she wasn't shaking with fear.

"You did." I put the gun down on the night table. I was feeling pretty sheepish myself. "You never know who might be dropping in," I said by way of explanation. It probably seemed like a pretty lousy explanation to her.

"That's a real gun, isn't it?"

"It ain't a toy." Through sleepy eyes, I looked her over. She was wearing a short silk robe, filling it out very nicely.

"Guns scare me," she said.

"Guns aren't so bad. It's bullets you have to watch out for." I was surprising myself with my own cleverness. Usually, I need a couple of cigarettes and a cup of coffee just to kick over my engine.

She undid the tie on her robe and let it fall to the floor. Just like in the movies. I was staring, but she didn't seem to mind. I had a feeling she was used to it.

"Well," she said, "I hope you're not that quick on the draw in bed."

Uh-huh.

"Come on in and find out."

There's nothing like sex in the A.M., if you ask me. It's better when you top it off with bacon and eggs, coffee and toast. By the time we were finished frolicking, I had worked up a pretty good appetite. We went downstairs to the dining room and found Nate already taking advantage of the cook Arnold Long kept on twenty-four-hour alert.

Naturally, I would have preferred to take a little extra batting practice with Marla, but we had places to go and people to find. Nate lost the coin flip, so he drew Reverend Whitey. I won a date with Cindi West and the People's Book Store. Steve Farrell's place was in that neighborhood, and if time permitted, I wanted to have a look around Sherri's apartment.

Walters brought in some of the other notes from People Against Pornography, and we subjected them to amateur handwriting analysis. It's hard to evaluate printing, but we were inclined to believe the letters were the work of different people. Unfortunately, neither Walters nor Arnie Long knew the location of Reverend Whitey's church. Sometimes it pays to take these cranks a little more seriously.

I decided to call my friend Rolf Laxman, an editor at *Chicago's American*, to see if he knew anything about Whitey Howard. Mindi stopped me.

"Are you trying to find out where he lives?" she asked as I picked up the phone. "I can tell you that."

"How do you know where he lives?" Nate asked.

Mindi giggled. "We went over there—some of the girls and a few of the guys—it was back in May, I think. This guy Oscar, he works in the mailroom. He saw Reverend Whitey one day and followed him back there. Oscar knew him from when he comes around here. We thought it would be funny to go over and march in front of *his* place for a change."

"Very good," Nate said.

"There were about maybe ten of us. Sherri was there, too. That's how Sherri met Pablo in the first place. It's in a real crummy neighborhood, over on the West Side, near like Milwaukee and Division. I've got the address written down."

"What about Pablo?" Nate asked her. "What was he doing there?"

"I don't know. He was just hanging around outside. He was talking to us because we were protesting, you know? He thought it was funny. He and Sherri smoked a joint together. She told him to come by and see her. A few weeks later, he did."

Nate gave her a kiss. "You'd make a great detective, kiddo. Keep watching and listening."

I thought about going right after Pablo Johnson, but the Paradise Room was just a few blocks away on Clark Street. After my conversation with Marla the night before, I had a feeling Cindi West might know something. Besides, Arnie Long had said talking to her would be a waste of time. Over the years I've learned that you learn an awful lot by talking to the people your clients don't want you to talk to.

Cindi West was a looker, but she wasn't as pretty as the photos I'd seen of her younger sister. Marla was right about her weight. Her Cherub jumpsuit looked like it had been glued on, and she was going to need help peeling it off. Still, it was plain to see that if she lost fifteen pounds, Cindi would be a knockout.

It was quickly apparent that she was more committed to curbing amiability than to counting calories. I expected as much. She had cause to be bitter and no reason to cooperate with a private eye who was working for Long & Son.

"If you have a few extra minutes, would you stop over and see me?" I said, showing her my identification. That line never works without proper ID.

Sometimes it doesn't work with it. This appeared to be one of them.

"I never have a few minutes."

I looked around the restaurant. It was before the lunchtime rush, assuming there would be one. "Do you think you could make a couple? It's important."

She pointed toward the bar. "Have a drink. I'll think about it."

I had two and made small talk with Helene, the bar Cherub. She was a few years older than Cindi and far more affable.

"You a friend of Cindi's?"

"Not exactly. I'm just waiting to talk to her. I don't think she wants to talk to me."

"That's too bad for her. You'd be a step up in class from the other guys she hangs out with." She leaned in and lit my cigarette. "She goes for the hippie types. She's really a pretty nice kid. She's just been in kind of a bad mood lately."

I was ordering my third and beginning to feel like my old tired self when Cindi's nice-kid side began to reveal itself. Maybe she was impressed with my perseverance. Maybe she just wanted to get it over with and get rid of me.

She ushered me to a corner booth. "I've got to make a living, so you better make this fast."

"I'm looking for your sister. She's been missing for almost two weeks now."

Cindi sucked on a menthol cigarette—one of the long thin ones. "I talked to Arnie Long already. I'll tell you what I told him. I haven't seen her in three months."

"He told me you said you haven't seen her in six."

She rolled her eyes and sighed. "Three months, six months, what's the difference? I haven't seen her and I haven't talked to her since she disappeared. OK?"

"I take it you and she aren't exactly on friendly terms."

"Yeah, you catch on real fast. Sherri has one interest in life—Sherri. She doesn't care who she fucks over as long as she's happy."

"She sounds like a lovely person. You'd think she'd fit right in with the Paradise family. I wonder why things didn't work out."

Her expression changed slightly. I'd be stretching things to call it a smile, but it was a marked improvement over the sneer I'd seen so far. "So you've been to Eden, huh?" She pronounced the name of Arnold Long's estate with determined sarcasm. "And Sherri had a falling-out with the two assholes."

"Which assholes could you be referring to?"

She snickered. "Daddy Long and his retard son." She lit

another cigarette and took a long drag. "Oh, excuse me. I shouldn't be speaking so highly of your boss."

"He's paying me, that's all. Just like he's paying you. I take it you don't like them much."

"My, you *do* catch on fast. Actually, I love them both from the bottom of my heart. It's just that they happen to be the world's two lousiest lays."

"That's strange. I gather they get a lot of practice."

She snorted. "A lot of good it's done them. The old man can barely get it up, and his son shoots faster than Jesse James."

"You're speaking from personal experience, of course. About the Longs, not Jesse James." I was no match for Cindi West's cynicism, but irony is my middle name.

She chuckled a bit, then shrugged. "We all make mistakes."

"Why didn't they run your photos in the magazine?"

That one caught her off guard. "Jesus, you know everything, don't you? Why are you talking to me?"

"I'm looking for your sister." My voice was quiet but stern. Cindi acted tough, but I thought I might get her to come around a bit. I'd been told she was twenty-three, but she looked thirty.

"Cindi, where would Sherri go if she wanted to hide out?"

"Beats the hell out of me."

"Would she go to see Pablo Johnson?"

Cindi frowned. "Who's that?"

"A guy she was hanging out with lately. Arnold Long didn't like him."

"Sounds like he could be a good guy. Too bad I don't know him." She looked at her watch. "I've got to make a living again."

"You don't like working here. It's none of my business, but why do you do it?"

"You're right, it's none of your business. If you had a bunch of conventioneers trying to pinch your ass, you'd hate it, too. But I'll tell you, anyway. I make good money."

Cindi was standing up now. I made one last try.

"You must have some idea where your sister would go. Would you try to think?"

"Shit." She crushed out her cigarette. "Check with Steve Farrell. Steve and Sherri were pretty close."

"Were they lovers?"

"Hah! You're really an innocent guy, you know?" Cindi was smiling now, an authentic smile. "I kind of like that."

I tried to smile back, but I probably blushed instead. First a nice guy, now innocent. Pretty soon one of these girls was going to mistake me for a senior citizen.

"Steve fucked everyone," she said. "Every girl Steve shoots, Steve fucks." She paused, then answered a question I wasn't going to ask. "That's right. Including me."

"Arnie Long said Farrell told him he hadn't seen Sherri."

"That doesn't mean anything. If Sherri didn't want to talk to Long, Steve would cover for her. Besides, Steve doesn't answer to Arnie Long."

"Farrell doesn't like Arnie?"

"Hates his Ivy League guts. Hang around for a while. You won't meet anyone who likes Arnie Long. Except his father. And that's only out of obligation."

I walked with her toward the door. "Thanks. You've been a big help."

"Hah! That's a laugh."

But Cindi West wasn't laughing. "Listen," she said, "if you find Sherri and she really needs to talk to someone, tell her to call me. I can't stand the little bitch, but I wouldn't want anything to happen to her."

CHAPTER 7

People's Books was on Addison Street, half a block west of Wrigley Field. There was a ball game in progress by the time I got there. The Cubs, as I mentioned, were in first place, but they had lost three in a row. From the catcalls I heard booming out of the stadium, I figured they were in the process of dropping another one.

About a dozen hippie types were hanging outside the store. One of them passed me a leaflet that said FREE THE CHICAGO 8, JAIL NIXON, BRING THE WAR HOME. Fine by me.

The inside of the shop looked like someone had brought the war there. It was on the first floor of a two-flat that might well have been condemned. The floors were warped and rotting under the weight of tall stacks of newspapers, pamphlets and dust-covered books. The walls looked ready to crumble any minute, but someone had tried to hold them up by patching the cracks with posters. I recognized Stalin, Mao, Dylan and Joplin, but I still would have flunked if they were giving a quiz.

The ratio of workers to customers was one to one until I arrived. I'm not sure you'd count me as a customer, but if the guy behind the counter wanted to, it was OK with me. I thought the store might do a little more business if they added a line of baseball souvenirs.

The proprietor was older than I am—middle forties, maybe fifty. He was overweight and balding, and I had a feeling he hadn't been able to come to grips with the balding part. I say this because he had let the fringe grow out enough to make a pony tail. He was leaning back in a battered wooden chair and resting his feet up on the counter. His head was angled downward, and he was engrossed in some sort of radical newspaper. The pony tail rested on his left shoulder. It was secured with a clip that had a peace sign on it. I've questioned a lot of different types in my time, but this was new turf to me.

I walked straight to the counter and tapped my fingers on it to get his attention. No luck. I tapped harder, with my knuckles, until his feet began to vibrate.

"Yeah, can I help you?" He didn't look up from his paper.

"I hope so. I'm looking for a guy named Paul Johnson. You might know him as Pablo."

He continued to stare at the paper. "You a narc?"

"No, I'm not a narc. I was told Johnson works here."

"FBI or CIA?"

"Neither." I pulled out my ID and laid it on the counter. If he checked it, he must have done so while I blinked. "Do you know where Pablo is? I need to talk to him."

When at last he looked up, his gaze went right past me to the customer, a tall, slender longhair. "Listen, Mr. Narc. I really don't like people coming in here asking a lot of questions."

I was tempted to reach across the counter and teach him a few lessons in self-defense, but I opted for self-restraint. I've gotten less violent as I get older, and I'd feel pretty sheepish sucker-punching a guy with a peace sign in his pony tail.

He spoke now to the customer, who was reading a thick gray book with red letters on it. "By the time you're finished with that, the revolution's gonna be over, buddy."

The longhair turned and looked at me. He shrugged. I smiled and gave him a peace sign. I felt like I was beginning to get in the spirit of things.

I loosened my tie and walked to one of the book racks while the pony tail continued to act officious. "Why don't you take that book home or take a walk," he told the kid.

The kid chose the latter, but not before stopping in the doorway. "Fascist pig," he said.

I picked up the first book that caught my eye—*Imperialism: The Highest Stage of Capitalism*, by Lenin. I could feel him watching me as I examined the cover. Using his tactic, I held it up and spoke without looking at him. "Is this good?"

He took a moment to answer. "Depends on your politics."

I selected another, a big thick hardcover with an ugly typeface—*Stalin: Problems of Leninism*. "How about this one?"

I had his attention now. "What are you, a Stalinist or a Leninist?"

I shrugged. "I'm into Marx mostly. Leninism presents some problems for me." To add weight to my point, I held the heavy book aloft. "Do you have anything on anarchism?"

That one got him up and out of his chair. He came around the counter and lumbered to a rack across the room. He pulled out a bulging paperback and brought it to me. "Try this Bakunin book," he advised. "You might find this pretty interesting."

I added it to my pile and showed him a book by someone called Amacar Cabral. "I've heard this Cabral guy's pretty good," I said.

He nodded and reached across me to pull out a paperback called *Pedagogy of the Oppressed*. "If you're into the Third World movement, you might like this."

"Oh yeah, I am." I took it and started a new stack. "What about this guy Franz Fanon?" I was holding something called *The Wretched of the Earth*.

"Oh, that guy. Someone told me he died a couple years ago in Bethesda, Maryland. That's all I know about him."

"I have a cousin in Bethesda. Why don't you give me two copies."

I moved over to the magazine rack and started pulling out one of everything—*The Vanguard, The Militant, The Black Panther, Rising Up Angry, Chicago Seed.* I stacked them on the counter and went to get a handful more. I picked out posters of Marx, Lenin, Trotsky and Hendrix from a wastebasket with a hand-lettered sign that said HALF PRICE. As I stepped back to the counter, a tattered pamphlet caught my eye—*Oman and the*

Occupied Arab Gulf. "Great," I said, tossing it onto the pile. "I've been looking all over for this."

The aging hippie was grinning. "I get it. Red Squad."

"What?"

"C'mon, you can't be that dumb."

I apologized for my ignorance. If this guy didn't have a lot to say about Pablo Johnson, I was going to deck him for sure.

"The Red Squad. It's the Chicago police spy unit. Bunch of fascists."

"They all are." It's not my style to call people fascists, but I'd had some dealings with the Chicago police. Nice guys, they weren't. And that's coming from someone who used to be a New York cop.

I smiled my charming smile. "Now. What can you tell me about Pablo Johnson?"

He shrugged. "Everybody's looking for Pablo. What did he do now?"

"Other people have been asking about him?"

"Just one. Guy called here on the phone. Said he worked for *Paradise* magazine. I called him a pig and hung up."

"Bill Walters," I said.

"Yeah, that's the name. Sounded like a real asshole."

"I think you might get along with him." I was thinking of telling him it takes one to know one. Instead, I said, "You'd make an interesting dialectic."

He laughed at that. "You're not so bad for a suit."

"I need to talk to Pablo. Does he still work here?"

"Pablo never worked a day in his life. He didn't do any work here. He's an acid casualty. I fired him."

"Do you know where he lives? Does he have another job?"

The proprietor adjusted his pony tail clasp. I averted my eyes. "Someone told me they saw him selling hot dogs over at Wrigley Field. I don't know. I never knew where he lived. I think he might have been staying with some girl from that Paradise place. He was always talking about being down there. Every day he had some story about getting laid with one of those chicks. I never believed him. He was so full of shit." He shook his head, and the pony tail came lose again. "Hey, do you work for that Paradise place, too?"

I nodded. "They hired me to find the girl he was going out with."

"Shit. She's missing?" He shook his head. It seemed to be a sign he was thinking. "Are they offering a reward? I bet they'd be willing to pay an awful lot."

"Not officially. I bet it could be worth some money if you could help me find her."

"Shit. I met that chick once. Pablo brought her to a meeting. He wanted to convert her to the movement. She had no idea what we were talking about. I'll tell you one thing, though. She had great tits." He sighed and cupped his hands over his chest. "She had a sister, too, right?"

"Yeah. Did Pablo know her, too?"

"Hell, I don't know. He was so full of shit. I didn't even listen to him half the time. Get this: He changed his name to Pablo to be in solidarity with the Third World movement. Up to a few months ago, Pablo thought the Third World was an amusement park in Joliet. He always had some crazy fuckin' scheme. He wanted to buy half a million hits of acid and put 'em into the city water supply. He thought it would be real funny if the whole city was tripping. Great fuckin' idea, huh?"

I shook my head along with him. "What's your name?"

"Oh, sorry." He put out his hand. When I tried to clasp it, he hit me with some sort of secret shake. "Moses Godley."

I didn't ask whether it was his real moniker. "How long since you've seen Pablo?"

"I don't know. Three weeks, a month maybe. You know, we finally had to throw the jerk out of our study group."

"That so?" I didn't bother asking what serious offense he committed to merit such stern punishment.

Just then a frizzy-haired girl came in carrying a knapsack. Business was booming. Godley totaled up my purchase. It came to eighty-seven dollars. I gave him a Ben Franklin and told him to donate the balance to his favorite charity. He smiled and put it in his pocket. Then I handed him my card, with the Paradise phone number written on it.

"If Johnson comes in, call me right away."

"He's not coming back here, man," Moses said.

"What makes you so sure?"

"He ripped me off. Emptied the cash register at lunchtime and never came back."

"Well, if you hear anything about him, give me a call. I might stop by for some more books."

Godley handed me the newspaper he had been reading. "Take this with you," he said. "It's all about the demonstration next month."

It was called *New Left Notes*. The headline was almost too big to read at arm's length—BRING THE WAR HOME.

"They're calling it the four Days of Rage," Moses said. He gave me a peace sign. "I enjoyed rappin' with you, Mark. If you find Pablo, give him a shot for me. That asshole still owes me fourteen bucks."

"Sure thing."

I thought about asking him to mail me the books, then reconsidered. Outside, the ranks of the hippies had dwindled to four. As I carted my bags past them, I heard one of them mutter "Red Squad."

I didn't look back. I walked a block east to the corner of Addison and Clark, where a disheartened Cub fan was trying to bury himself under beer cans outside the Cubby Bear Lounge. I dropped a bag of books on each side of him.

He looked up at me through booze-fogged eyes. "Let's play two," he said.

CHAPTER 8

The Cubs were losing to the Mets 6-0 when I entered Wrigley Field. It was the fourth inning, and Tom Seaver hadn't given up a hit yet. There was a lot of groaning going on. The Cubs seemed certain of winning the pennant, but anything is possible. Just ask anyone from Philadelphia who followed the Phillies in 1964.

The bleachers were full, so I couldn't look for Pablo Johnson out there. But I did wander the upper and lower decks. No sign of him.

After a few inquiries of vendors and security types, I managed to find my way to the ballpark services office. I spoke with Charlie Bellows, the aptly named head of vendors. He had no trouble remembering Pablo Johnson and gave me a rundown in a volume usually reserved for hawking peanuts.

"Asshole. Total fuckin' asshole." He was chewing on the stub of a cigar that looked like it had been kicked around the floor of the men's john for a few innings. "We hired the jerk three weeks ago. He worked two, maybe three games. After that, I never saw him again. And I never wanna. I don't know how he got into the union. He musta knew somebody. It ain't a hard job, you know, sellin' hot dogs. This guy figured out a way to fuck it up."

"You wouldn't happen to know where he lives."

"No, sir. I was you, I'd try checkin' the psycho wards of the city hospitals."

I thanked Bellows for his time and made my way to the exit. Hordes of fans were doing the same. The Cubs had gotten to Seaver for a run, but the Mets had responded with two of their own.

It was only 2:30, so I decided to make another stop before returning to Eden. It turned out to be a good idea.

Steve Farrell lived in a high rise on Sheridan Road a block south of Belmont. It took me a minute of persistent buzzing to get an answer from him over the lobby intercom.

"What's buzzin', babe?" His voice sounded fuzzy through the twenty-five-cent speaker above the row of mailboxes.

"Mark Renzler. I'm a private investigator working for Arnold Long. I'd like to talk to you for a few minutes."

"What'd you say?"

I raised my voice. "I'm working for Arnold Long."

"I don't know anyone named Long."

"Sure you do. You work for him." I was shouting now. "I need to talk to you."

"Bye, bye. Have a nice trip."

I thought about putting a bullet through the lock. Instead, I ran my hand over all the apartment buzzers and stationed myself at the speaker box. Within seconds there were eight or ten voices talking at me.

"Exterminator." One of them had to have bugs.

Apparently, quite a few of them did. The security door buzzed for close to a minute. By that time I was standing at the elevators, waiting for a lift to Steve Farrell's floor, the fourteenth.

The photographer took plenty of time answering the door. I used it to get my foot ready.

It only took one kick. From there I used my hand.

Farrell sprawled backward onto the floor. He looked scared. He should have been. I was mad.

He reached for an ashtray on the table behind him.

"If you throw it, you eat it." I took two steps forward and smiled for effect.

He was a small guy, probably five feet seven inches. He wore jeans with frayed edges, no shirt. He had a full head of hair but none on his chest. He moved back on hands and knees as I advanced. I didn't know what drug he was on, but it looked pretty powerful.

"Who are you? What do you want?" The smugness I'd heard in the lobby had vanished from his voice. Fear had taken its place.

"I already told you. I'm working for Arnold Long. What are you on, acid?"

He began grinning, then he laughed. I didn't know what was so funny.

"Are you kidding? I don't touch acid. Never. Mescaline's the way, man. Where you been?"

I might have requested an explanation of the distinction, but I was distracted by a voice coming from behind the sofa. It was a girl's voice. It had a spooky quality about it. Psychotic or drugged, maybe both.

"Steve, can I come out now? Is it safe?"

"Sure, babe, come on out. It's just some guy that thinks we're doing acid."

Sherri West wasn't wearing anything when she crawled out from behind the sofa. Not unless paint has become a type of outerwear in the psychedelic age. It was mostly orange paint, but there were a few black stripes. It was a nice contrast.

She began to claw at the rug. "I'm a tiger. I'm king of the jungle." As proof, she growled at me.

Farrell laughed. He was still on all fours. "It's the lion that's king of the jungle, Sherri. Besides, you're a chick. You'd be queen of the jungle."

Sherri looked up at me and grinned. "Who are you?"

"I'm the zoo keeper."

They looked at each other and laughed. Then Sherri's face got serious. "Are you really the zoo keeper, mister?"

I tried to smile but couldn't. I walked to the sofa and sat down. Moses Godley was right. Sherri West did have great tits. And no body hangup.

"Arnold Long sent me. He's worried about you, Sherri."

"No he's not." Still on her knees, she stretched her arms over her head and clawed at the air. "He's a bastard. I should scratch his eyes out. Grrrowl!"

"He wants you to come back to Eden. Your magazine's coming out in two weeks. You're supposed to go on a publicity tour."

I couldn't tell from the vacant expression on her face whether Sherri understood what I was saying.

"You're wrong," she said. "I'm in another magazine."

"No. You're in *Paradise*, the October issue. Do you know what I'm talking about?"

"You don't know what *you're* talking about, Mr. Zoo Keeper." She was giggling now and flat on her back. I thought about grabbing her and carrying her out, but where would I take her? Not back to Arnold Long. To the emergency room of a hospital maybe.

"She's right, man," Farrell said. "We're not with *Paradise*."

"What? Arnie Long said you told him you hadn't seen Sherri. How long has she been here?"

"I don't know. What day is it?" Farrell and Sherri started to laugh again.

I was about ready to pick him up and shake him. "Why didn't you tell Long she was with you?"

"Man, we've been trying to tell you. We're not with those assholes anymore. I'll show you."

Farrell began shuffling through a pile of papers on the coffee table. Sherri was now sitting Indian style. It was a great position, but I tried not to look.

Farrell handed me a sheet of legal-size paper. It was printed on both sides. It was an interesting document. I don't have any patience for legal mumbo jumbo, but as the song says, you don't need a weatherman to tell you which way the wind blows.

I looked over the contract, then looked at Farrell. "Let me get this straight. You've signed a contract with *Nook*?"

Farrell grinned. "That's right, man."

I looked at Sherri. She was laughing again. She leaned back on the floor, arms pinned beneath her. Her legs were raised and slightly spread. At one time she must have taken a yoga class. I thought of a joke I had heard the week before. It was a lousy joke. The punch line had something to do with a taco.

"I'm no Angel, I'm a Nookie. I'm no Angel, I'm a Nookie." She was half talking, half singing. It sounded like a Gregorian chant. Maybe she'd taken a music appreciation course, too.

"This is crazy," I said to Farrell. But it was all fitting together. "Long will go to court."

"Man, you just jam my head. The lawyers checked it out. I own the photos, man. *Paradise* fucked up. In fact, they still have to pay me for the photos they use."

"What? Are you kidding?"

"Well, I may be wrong about that. But I own the outtakes."

"This is great," I said. "Were you planning on telling Arnold Long?"

"Oh sure, man. I would've told him. But I don't mind. You can tell him if you want."

"Thanks a lot."

I asked Farrell for a copy of the contract. He had one filed in the bathroom. Sherri practiced her yoga while he went to get it. She was in an advanced position now. It was going to take an advance of time before I forgot it.

"Hey, mister, do you think I'll make a good Nookie or what?"

"The best," I said. "No question about it."

Farrell returned with the contract. "Thanks a lot, man. You're saving me a lot of trouble."

"Don't mention it."

I turned to Sherri and spoke to her in a stern voice. "When you get back from Mars, call your sister. Even she's worried about you."

Sherri and her photographer looked at each other. I didn't understand what the look meant. I didn't understand anything.

CHAPTER 9

Marla was standing sentry when I returned to Eden at 4:30. Nate, she said, was back in the Fountain Room with Mindi. She led me there via a route that bypassed the Sanctuary. I gave her a kiss and asked if she was free for dinner. She answered in the affirmative.

The Fountain Room was called the Fountain Room because there was a large fountain in the middle of it. There was an even larger bar. I walked straight to it and got myself a double Old Grand-Dad. Nate and Mindi were sitting in a corner booth. He had one hand on her waist and the other wrapped around a drink. I overheard them talking as I approached.

"Is it my imagination, or do all you girls have names that end in *i*?" he was asking.

"Silly. Marla's name doesn't end in *i*."

I didn't think I was interrupting anything heavy, so I slid right in across from them.

"Ah, Brother Renzler," Nate said. "You're looking rather sickly o'er the pale cast of thought."

"Interesting you should say that," I said. "I was just thinking about Shakespeare a little while ago myself."

"*Midsummer Night's Dream*, I hope."

"Uh-uh. *Hamlet*. Who do you want to be—Rosencrantz or Guildenstern?"

"Bad news?"

"Sort of. Tell me about your day first." I lit a cigarette. It was a Camel. I used to smoke them all the time, but I had finally heeded the surgeon general's warnings and switched to filters the year before. After my encounter with Sherri West and Steve Farrell, I decided to treat my lungs to something really poisonous.

"It turns out that the Reverend Whitey Howard, self-appointed guardian of morality and truth, has moved his church," Nate said. "From one seedy neighborhood to another. But I found it. Had to bribe one of his old neighbors to tell me where it was. It sounds like he had a lot of traffic going in and out of there. Now he's down near Chicago Stadium. It's a great location. Unfortunately, the church was closed when I got there."

"Were you able to get inside?"

"Oh yes. Through the rear entrance. He's got a little print shop in the back room. It's not the latest in technology, but it gets the job done."

He pulled a few tattered pamphlets out of his jacket pocket and tossed them to me. They were of even lower quality than the ones I had purchased at People's Books.

"It's quite a place," Nate said. "Almost as nice as your apartment."

"Thanks a lot. Did you talk to the man?"

"Well, he was busy giving spiritual counseling to a couple of young men, but I beseeched him for a few moments of his valuable time. He obliged me under the threat of corporal punishment."

"How young were they?"

"Old enough to be legal. Young enough to be in decidedly bad taste. They still had their clothes on when I got there."

"What did he have to say about the letters to Sherri?"

"He denied everything. He admitted it was his stationery, but he insisted someone must have stolen it. Said he would never stoop to such tactics."

"Do you believe him?"

"I suppose so. Who knows with a lunatic? He did admit to sending notes to the other girls."

Nate leaned his head in and raised his eyebrows. "But I got the impression Reverend Whitey has done quite a bit of stooping in his day."

"Yes?"

"The front of Reverend Whitey's church—the vestibule, if you will—is lined with photos of young men. I assume it's kind of an honor roll of spiritual-counseling graduates." He pulled a black-and-white snapshot from his shirt pocket. "I think this fellow must have graduated cum laude. There was also a color picture of him. It was framed."

I looked at the photo. It was old, but it had to be the same person. His hair was shorter then, of course, and I'd guess he was about ten years younger. But Paul "Pablo" Johnson looked a little deranged even back then.

"Opens up some interesting possibilities, don't you think?"

I nodded. "Sure does. But I'm afraid I managed to close them up."

"What does that mean?"

I gave him the abridged version, promising the details for a later time, if he still wanted to hear them.

Nate put his arm around Mindi. "Shit. I was really getting to like it here."

I shrugged. "We don't necessarily have to go back right away."

Mindi agreed. "You can stay for a few more days."

Nate smiled and shook his head. "Methinks after our visitation with Arnold Long, we just might not want to."

Bill Shakespeare couldn't have said it any better.

CHAPTER **10**

Arnold Long appeared to be in a splendid mood when Nate and I marched into the Sanctuary behind Arnie Long and Bill Walters. You'd be in a good mood, too, if you were being molested by the towel blondes during normal business hours.

Of course, his mood changed—suddenly.

I skipped the stuff about Pablo Johnson and Cindi West and only alluded momentarily to Nate's encounter with Reverend Whitey Howard. That would go in my official report (and probably never be read).

Arnold was off the surgical table in a mad rage almost as quickly as I felt the last syllable of Len Wyder's name dribble out of my mouth. Of course, I did mention the name at the end of a long sentence that began with a clause about Sherri West opting for Nookiedom over Angelhood.

He stepped to the floor with such suddenness that the towel blondes were unable to prevent his only garment from falling to his ankles. He kicked the towel angrily, sending it sailing across the room in an arc that ended at the intersection of Bill Walters' shoulders and neck. He turned to face the girls, his manhood in open view of anyone who dared to look. I averted my eyes.

"My robe!" he shrieked. "Bring me my robe!"

I found it curious that the Bard of Paradise began to exhibit symptoms of body hangup at a moment when he was otherwise out of emotional control. But I had little time to mull the implications, because he was already interrogating me with staccato rapacity.

"How's Sherri? Is she OK?"

I nodded. "She was high on drugs, but she's alive and well."

"Sherri on drugs?"

"Yessir. Mescaline, I believe."

"Farrell says he owns the photos?"

"I'm afraid so. I have the contract—"

"Lemme see that damn thing." Arnold stepped forward to take the document, pulling one of the towel blondes with him. She was trying to put his robe on without obtrusion. He pushed her away with his arm. "Get away from me. I can dress myself."

He snatched the contract from my hand and squinted at it. "Where are my glasses, goddamnit?"

"Now, Dad, don't get upset. There must be some mistake."

"Don't tell me how to behave." Arnold was behind his fig leaf desk now and giving it to his son with both barrels. "What do you know about legal matters? Nothing! What do you know about anything? Nothing!"

Arnie's face turned tomato red and he tried to force a sheepish grin. I glanced at Nate. He was trying to suppress one.

One of the blondes got up the courage to hand Arnold his eyeglasses. He used them to put a dent in the contract, which he had thrown disgustedly on the desk. The frames snapped.

"I can't make sense of this trash," he muttered. He flipped a switch on his desk intercom and barked into it. "Get me Len Wyder on the phone right away."

His order was answered by the tentative voice of a woman who had not been lucky enough to watch the proceedings. "Do you mean the man who's publishing that new magazine?"

"Don't ask questions. Just do what I say." Arnold turned and spoke to Walters. "The legal department. I want them all down here. Right now."

The PR man nodded obediently, then turned on his heels and sprinted from the room. I went to the nearest bar to mix drinks. Long saw me. "Triple scotch, Renzler. Neat."

The female voice came back through the box as Long took the drink with two trembling hands. "Mr. Wyder is on the line."

Arnold flipped a switch and leaned over the phone. He began to speak at life-threatening volume. "Wyder! You asshole!"

The voice that answered was slimy, the sort you hear hooting after hookers on Eighth Avenue. "Arnold, baby. How ya doin' there, buddy?"

"Don't give me that buddy crap, Wyder. What's this nonsense about Steve Farrell working for you?"

"It ain't nonsense, buddy." Wyder snickered. "I got your boy *and* your goy." The publisher of *Nook* must have had a phone box in his office, because we could hear background laughter with what sounded like female intonation.

"You'll never get away with this, asshole."

Wyder responded as if he were reading a rehearsed script. I had a feeling he had been waiting for Arnold's call for a while now. "Read the contract, buddy. I snatched your snatch, fair and square."

Long grimaced. I could see veins bulging blue on his temples. They reminded me of rivers on a road atlas. I wondered if Arnold was the sort of guy who disdains the annual checkup.

"You won't get away with this, scumbag," he roared. "You don't fuck Arnold Long and live to tell about it."

"Aw c'mon, buddy. Calm down. You may be Long, but I'm Wyder. Ha, ha!"

"That's right, keep laughing, asshole," Long yelled. "But mark my words. I'll run you and your ugly tramp of a daughter right out of this town."

The female, presumably Wyder's ugly tramp of a daughter, added her two cents in a voice that sounded like a cement mixer. "Arnold, I've just been dying to tell you. Sherri West has a luscious set of lips. Yum, yum."

"Shut up, you homely bulldyke bitch."

Wyder's daughter let out a husky laugh. "Say hi to Arnie for me."

"Urrrgh!" Arnold swung his arm against the phone, knocking it off the desk. It landed at Arnie's feet. The plastic casing had shattered, but damn if the guts of the thing weren't still working.

Wyder's obnoxious voice came through loud and clear. "Good talkin' with you, buddy. Maybe we can stop by for a potable sometime soon."

Arnie smartly put an end to the call by disconnecting the switch with his foot. His father turned from the desk and walked slowly to the pool table at the far end of the room. He picked up a pool cue and studied it in his hands. Suddenly, he wheeled and swung the cue along a row of cordial glasses behind one of the bars. As Bill Walters and the Paradise legal staff arrived, they were confronted with the spectacle of their boss holding a pool cue over his head. His expression was vacant but menacing. I hoped the company fringe benefits included health insurance.

Long stalked toward the front of the room. His robe, which I failed to mention previously was white satin festooned with fig leaves of varying sizes and colors, had come unbelted. He held the pool cue in front of him, gripping tightly, as if he were a tightrope walker trying to maintain his balance. He spoke now in a more reasonable volume, by which I mean that he probably was within FAA noise safety levels for an industrial zone.

"Who's the photo editor around here this week?" he asked Walters.

"Dave Young," the PR man answered.

"Did you get him?"

"Well, no. I thought—"

"Don't think. Get Young. Now!"

Walters did a pirouette and darted from the room, leaving the four lawyers to retreat in choreographed terror as their boss advanced on them. He stopped about one pool cue's length away.

"Bring me the contract."

Arnie Long and one of the towel blondes collided at the desk while carrying out orders. Blood won out over beauty, and Arnie managed to slip the paper into his father's outstretched hand without drawing any insults.

Arnold handed the document to the nearest attorney, a short, thin fellow with graying hair. "Tell me what this says," he growled. "And I want it in English, not lawyer talk."

The man's hands were trembling as he began reading. I would have felt sorry for him, if I didn't harbor a long-standing dislike for lawyers that dates back to Little League baseball when Ernie Feldman's father was my coach.

Just then, Walters bounded into the room, and the attorney took the opportunity to pass the contract to one of his colleagues for a second opinion.

"Young's out on location at a photo shooting," the PR man reported.

"He's going to be the victim of a shooting next time I see him." Arnold paused. "No. I don't even want to see him. Clean out his office. Call him tonight and tell him he's fired."

"Are you serious?" Walters stammered.

"Do I look serious?"

The portly publisher was chewing on an unlit cigar that he had discovered moments before in the pocket of his robe. I already noted the garment's sporty design. He was wielding a pool cue in his left hand. If you stood at the right angle, you could get a bird's eye view of his middle-aged manhood without even trying to look. Bill Walters was standing at the right angle. I hoped he wasn't dumb enough to answer the question truthfully.

He started to speak, stopped, then did another one-eighty and headed out of the room. Smart thinking.

Long turned to face the lawyer. By this time, three of them had perused the contract.

"Well?" he demanded.

"It, uh, looks like a perfectly legal document, I'm sorry to say."

"You should be sorry. You just lost your job."

The thin man avoided Long's death stare by looking at his feet.

"You're Weinstein, right?"

"No, sir, I'm Rosen."

"OK, you're fired, Rosen," Long said. Then, without irony, he added, "Sorry about the mixup with the name."

A chubby, balding fellow beside Rosen worked up the nerve to speak. "Excuse me, Mr Long."

I thought it was a peculiar opening, because the only thing he was interrupting was deadly silence. But I couldn't blame him under the circumstances.

"What?"

"I'd have to check our files, but it appears to me that this agreement only has applicability as regards the outtakes. I believe we may be able to run the photos of Sherri West in our October issue without untoward ramifications."

"*May* be able to run the photos!" Long was back in violation of federal safety standards. "Of course we're going to run the goddamn photos. The magazine's already printed. Isn't that right, Arnie?"

Arnie answered with a solemn nod.

"What's your name? Are you Weinstein?"

"No, sir, I'm Gross."

"You're fired, Gross."

"Dad, Dad!" Arnie's attempt to stop the massacre was futile.

Dad pointed his cigar at the next attorney in line, a tall, heavyset guy with thick-rimmed glasses. "What's your name?" he demanded.

"I'm Weinstein," the man said, grinning. I figured he either had a sense of humor or an outside income.

"You're fired, Weinstein." Arnold steadied himself on the pool cue and lit the cigar. He eyed his final victim, a much younger fellow with orange hair who looked like he was fresh out of law school.

"And what about you?" the publisher asked.

"Mike Murphy, Mr. Long." He extended his hand, but Arnold ignored it or didn't notice.

"Murphy!" Arnold turned to face his chip off the old block. "Arnie, what the hell are we doing with a mick lawyer? How many times have I told you that Jews make the best lawyers?"

Arnie threw up his hands and whined with exasperation. "But, Dad, you just fired all our Jewish lawyers!"

Arnold blew out a cloud of smoke. "You've got a point there, Arnie." He looked at the young attorney. "How long have you been here, Murphy?"

"Four months, Mr. Long."

"OK, you stay. I'm putting you in charge of the legal department. The first thing I want you to do is find out which photos we own, which we don't, which we can use and so forth. I'll want a full report tomorrow at noon."

Murphy looked sheepishly at his former colleagues, then nodded. "No problem, Mr. Long," he said.

Long dropped the cue and rebelted his robe. "All right, everyone out. I want my privacy." He turned abruptly and began walking to the far end of the room. He stopped at the edge of the pool, and I half expected him to hurl himself in. "I'm the laughing stock of the industry," I heard him mutter.

I wasn't sure which industry he was talking about. I'd never thought of girlie magazines as an industry.

As we reached the doorway, Long shouted my name. I turned to face him, but remained silent.

"You and Moore have done an excellent job, Renzler. Thank you."

"Don't mention it," I answered. "Just sorry that it turned out so bad for you."

"It's not your fault." He waved at the air with his cigar. "You know, I was serious about that director of security position. If you want the job, it's yours."

I stifled a laugh. "Thanks. I'll think it over."

Arnold spoke to his son. "Spread the word, Arnie. No party tonight."

"Yes, Dad. Are you OK?"

"I'm swell, Arnie. Just fucking swell."

Arnie swallowed the remains of his last dumb question, then escorted Nate and me down the hall as far as his office. "I'm sorry about Dad," he said.

"No need to apologize," I assured him. "We get to see some pretty weird stuff."

"Yeah, don't worry about it," Nate added. "I haven't seen a performance that good since Nixon lost the California governor's race in sixty-two."

When we got to his office, Arnie shook our hands. "You have

done a good job," he said. "I want you to feel welcome to stay here tonight."

"Thanks. We intend to." I was already thinking about my date with Marla. "But if it's all the same to you, I think we'll eat out tonight."

CHAPTER 11

It turned out to be a pleasant evening. Nate and I took the girls to a restaurant off Rush Street that claimed to have the best prime rib in Chicago. If you swallowed that line, you'd probably choke on the check, but I didn't think it was worth beefing about. After all, Aronld Long was picking up the tab.

Thanks, Arnold.

I hadn't expected to be leaving so soon, and I wouldn't have minded going to Wrigley Field on Saturday and Sunday to see if the Mets could knock off the Cubs a couple of more times. But twenty-four hours in Arnold Long's tree house was enough for any normal man. The place may have been the best wet dream a kid ever had, but I wasn't a kid anymore and I never much enjoyed the mess you had to deal with afterward, anyhow.

The evening did have one surprise, though it hardly seems worth mentioning compared with the day's other events. I had the impression that Arnie Long, like his dad, rarely left the complete living environment of Eden. But as we were exiting the restaurant, there was Arnie, chatting it up with a ratty-looking woman over a little eye of the prime. I waved to him, but he didn't seem to see me. Actually, he seemed like he was trying *not* to see me. All of which was OK by me. I didn't have much to say to him, either.

Sleep is what the doctor ordered, but I was able to do very well without in the presence of a wonder drug like Marla. I know it sounds corny, but the sweet young thing made me feel like, well, a new man. When I woke up in the morning, I'd still have my smoker's cough and less hair on my head than I went to bed with. But once in a while, it sure is nice to feel like you've turned back the clock.

Long after we had stopped making the bed shake, rattle and roll, I was lying awake in the dark, chain-smoking cigarettes and listening to the sound of Marla's breathing. Feeling young again made me think about my first wife, Amy. We met in 1953, two lovesick kids. I was still a cop then, three years out of City College. One of these days I just might go back there and graduate. We got married in 1954, divorced in '58. I could describe Amy in detail, but as I lay there, no matter how hard I tried, I could not picture her face.

The second time around was in '64. Kathy O'Leary. We were on the four-year plan, too. I didn't have any trouble picturing Kathy—and not just because I had seen her the week before. She was a classic Irish beauty, right down to her freckled pug nose. She also had a classic Irish temper, which flared after three drinks. For Kathy, three drinks was just warming up.

I've concluded that private eyes make lousy husbands. Their wives never know when they'll be home. Never know *if* they'll be home. When you're working, the hours suck; if you're not working, the money sucks. When you cross a private eye with a bartender, the only thing you can get is trouble. Kathy and I had lots of it. She still does. It's amazing we were able to last until '68. I figure it must have been mutual stubbornness.

As I finally began to doze off, I thought about the only other important woman in my life—excluding Mom and my sister, of course. The woman I should have married. Melissa Kramer.

When I met her in 1960, she had a job as a reporter at *The New York Times* and a marriage that was on the rocks. I helped it go over the edge and helped keep her from going over with it. We were the best of friends and the best of lovers. We never talked about marriage, except to agree what a rotten concept it was. When she took a job overseas, I suppose I could have gone with her. She almost came right out and asked me to. But I didn't think private detectives were much in demand in Rome. More than that, I guess I didn't want to follow Melissa halfway around the world to find out it wouldn't work.

I saw her when she came back to New York, but I never went to Rome to see her. We wrote lots of letters. On October 10, 1964, I got one that said she had changed her thinking about the concept of marriage. Falling in love will do that. I remember the date, because I read the letter after watching Ken Boyer hit a grand-slam home run in the World Series. The Yankees lost to the Cardinals, and I lost Melissa to a handsome, swarthy Italian. She didn't tell me he was handsome and swarthy—that's just the way I think of Italian men. A couple of years later, I met him and confirmed my suspicions. We don't write to each other much anymore.

That night, I headed out to McCabe's bar with the intention of getting pig-stinking drunk. I was about halfway to my goal when the new night bartender came on duty.

Her name was Kathy O'Leary.

I was dreaming about Kathy ringing out the cash register at McCabe's when the phone call woke me up at eight o'clock on Saturday morning. I was feeling like my old self again, which is to say old and tired. But Bill Walters must have passed the night alone, because his voice was booming and cheery.

"Yeah, Walters," I managed in response to his greeting. "How's Arnold feeling this morning?"

"I don't know and frankly I don't care."

"Indeed." This was not the Bill Walters I had come to know and dismiss.

"I need to speak with you and Nate before you leave town. When are you going?"

"I thought you were making all the arrangements," I said, taking a cigarette and a kiss on the forehead from Marla.

Walters chuckled. "Sorry, guy. That's not my job. I'm not working at Paradise anymore."

"What?" It takes a lot to get my attention in the morning, but this one definitely took me by surprise. "Did Long fire you, too?"

"Oh, no. Nothing like that. I left on my own. Found another job."

"Let me guess."

Walters laughed again. "That's right, Renzler. I have to tell you. Len Wyder's a helluva guy. I'd like you fellas to meet him before you leave Chicago. He'd like to meet you. I think we're going to need your services."

"I don't think—"

"Don't say no, yet. Believe me, there's a lot of dough in it for you. They're paying me a good buck over here. If you just pack up your bags and stop over for a little while, I'll see that you get back to New York on Len's plane."

"He's got one of them, too?"

"You bet. How about ten thirty?"

"Listen, Walters. I think there might be a conflict of interest—"

"Oh, no. There's no conflict. You'll see. All you have to do is talk to Len. You don't have to take the job." He paused. "Maybe you'd do it as a personal favor to me."

Oh, sure. Bill Walters was not at the top of the list of people for whom I wanted to perform personal favors. But damn if he hadn't talked me into it. Or maybe I was just in that good a mood.

"Oh, hell, OK. Where do you want to meet?"

"You'll do it? Great! I told him you would. We'll meet over here, at the Nook. It's on Sedgewick just below Armitage."

"The Nook?"

"Yeah, that's what Len calls his house. It's a dynamite place."

"I'll bet." I crushed out the cigarette. Now, for a little coffee.

CHAPTER 12

Eden was about as lively as the county morgue when Marla and I went downstairs to the breakfast room. I didn't know if the residents were in the habit of sleeping late on Saturdays or if they were suffering withdrawal from a night without a party.

Nate and Mindi arrived shortly after we did, and we poured ourselves full of coffee and smoked a dozen cigarettes before marshaling the energy to pack our bags. The girls gave us a ride to the Nook, kissed us goodbye and promised to hitch a ride to New York on the *Paradise 666* as soon as they could.

I wouldn't have known what to expect the Nook to look like, if I hadn't spent two days at Arnold Long's estate. It was a low-budget version of the same fantasy. Another great tree house, but built of used lumber.

It appeared that Len Wyder had a smaller staff than Long, but it *was* Saturday morning. There were two girls stationed in the front hall, both attired in tight-fitting black leather jumpsuits. They were comely but, well, a bit trashy compared with Marla, Mindi and the other ladies of Eden.

The comelier of the two leather girls said the phone was on the blink and went off to retrieve Bill Walters. The other, who had winked at Nate rather violently, strutted off to the rest room to repair a broken false eyelash. In the absence of other ambassadors, we took the liberty of wandering the premises.

The hallways at the Nook had the same labyrinthine quality as

Eden, but they were more brightly lit. This was a serious error of artistic judgment. Where the walls at Arnold Long's place were covered with photos of Paradise Angels from years gone by, Len Wyder's collection consisted mainly of giant erotic paintings done in the sparkled style that you see at Polish banquet halls and department store clearance sales. Being a painter, Nate took particular offense at this design element. And though my sense of art does not exceed the ability to recognize primary and secondary colors, I can tell quality from crap.

There was no quality on the walls of the Nook.

We continued to a bend in the hall, where we admired an impressionistic fornication scene involving large, disfigured organs set against an enormous pastel sunset. The title of the work was *Is There Sex After Holocaust?* I think I got the symbolism.

There was no sign of the leather girls or Bill Walters, but we could hear some sounds coming from a room about twenty-five feet ahead of us. They were strange sounds. I don't do them justice by saying that they reminded me of some seals I had seen a few months back when I took my nephew to the Bronx Zoo. After a brief exchange of baffled looks, Nate and I quickened our pace. The door to the room was open a crack, so I pushed it further ajar and peered inside.

With some regrets.

It was a little like opening Pandora's box—only weirder. I'll admit to a little body hangup, but I'm no boy scout, either. The scene we stumbled upon was a genuine heart-stopper.

There were three women. Two were wearing the black leather suits. The other was in her birthday suit. The uniformed girls were standing, the woman in the birthday suit was lying face down on a bed. Well, not a bed exactly, but the frame and springs to one. The birthday girl's arms and legs were spread. Her hands and feet were shackled to the corners of the frame. She had big feet. She was a big girl.

They weren't playing pin the tail on the donkey, unless the game has changed drastically since I last played it. The leather girls were holding straps. From the red marks on the birthday girl's buttocks, I could see that the straps were being used to teach her a little discipline. It looked like a lot of discipline to me.

I would have shut the door, said a Hail Mary and strolled right out of the Nook if Nate hadn't stepped inside. His mouth was agape and his eyes were bulging. One of my eyes is glass, but I bet you couldn't have told which one just then. Except for the occasional anecdote about Teresa of Avila, this was not the sort of thing you learn about in Catholic school. You do get to see more strange shit in my line of work, but this one definitely made my all-time top ten.

The attendants laid their straps on the birthday girl's ass, which was about the size of the earth in the Holocaust painting. She let out a series of groans that solved the mystery of the seal sounds. I would have intervened, but it was somehow clear that the antics were her idea.

Before we could make our exit, one of the disciplinarians spotted us and said, "Someone's here. Should we stop?"

The birthday girl twisted into an unnatural position to try to get a look at us. From my angle, I couldn't see her face. I made no effort to get a better view.

"Who are you?" Her voice had a familiar grating of huskiness, but that might have been my imagination.

I thought about saying I was the Roto-Rooter man, but my own pipes were clogged at the moment. Nate did the talking.

"We're looking for Len Wyder's office," he managed.

"This isn't it. But you're welcome to stay. I've got nothing against boys."

"We've had ours this morning," Nate answered. "Maybe another time."

"I hope so, big guy."

Uh-huh.

We got out of there fast. As we turned the corner, I bumped into Bill Walters, knocking him to the floor. He picked himself up, shook our hands, called us each buddy and thanked us for coming. Then he looked askance at the doorway behind us.

"Uh, you guys didn't go in there, did you?"

We admitted our guilt. It was real guilt.

The PR man shook his head and chuckled. "Pretty weird, wouldn't you say?"

Nate nodded solemnly. "Real fucking weird, Walters. I hope this guy Wyder keeps his pool cues under lock and key."

Walters smiled nervously. "Let's go to his office," he said, pointing down the hall.

"It's none of my business, Walters," I said. "But do you think this move over to *Nook* might be a step down in class for you?"

He sighed. "Yeah, I'm afraid so. What I'd really like to do is get a job over at *Playboy*. But I hear they check your references real carefully, if you know what I mean."

I nodded. In a strange sort of way, I was getting to like Walters.

"But," he added, "they're paying me a good buck over here. A real good buck."

I thought Nate was going to ask how much, but instead he said, "I sure the fuck hope so. You're going to need it to pay the psychiatrist's bills."

We turned right at the end of the long hall. Immediately around the corner was a bright red door with a large, wooden sign like you see at restaurants with nautical themes at the Jersey shore. Burned into the wood was the name of the room—THE NICHE.

Walters paused before he turned the doorknob. "By the way," he said. "I wouldn't make any comments about what you saw in the other room to Len. That was his daughter, Faith."

Suspicions confirmed. This was going to be a very short meeting.

CHAPTER **13**

The publisher of *Nook* magazine was being worked over by a black-haired girl with large breasts when we entered the Niche. She wore tight leather pants, lots of makeup and nothing else. Unlike his daughter, Wyder took his punishment sitting up and with no restraints on his limbs. His claim to be Wyder than Arnold Long would have been easy to verify even if he *had* been wearing a shirt.

"Renzler, glad to meet you," he said, rising from his stool and padding toward Nate with his hand outstretched.

Walters corrected the mistake with the smooth assurance of a man who was born to do PR, then went to the bar to mix us a "potable" at Wyder's urging.

The Niche offered essentially the same amenities as Arnold Long's Sanctuary, only on a smaller scale. The room was about one-third the size of Long's. There was one of everything Long had, except there were stools instead of surgical tables and a whirlpool bath instead of a wading pool. The desk, naturally, was not shaped like a fig leaf, but constructed of nautical wood that matched the sign on the door.

This was chosen, we soon found out, because the irrevocable course of Len Wyder's distinguished career had been charted thirty-two years ago on his eighteenth birthday, when he signed up to be a merchant marine. The rest, according to Wyder, was history, but that didn't stop him from explaining the events in more detail than I care to go into. It seemed to me that he could just as easily have made his millions in scrap metals, except that one of the regular features planned for his new magazine was a column devoted to seamen.

When it became apparent that Wyder was oblivious to our growing impatience, I decided to steer him back on course.

"This is all very interesting, Len," I said, "but what does it have to do with us?"

"Oh, I get it. You guys are the type that like to get right down to business."

I answered him with a nod.

He reached around and patted his topless attendant on the ass. "Run along, Honey. Time for shop talk. If you see Faith, send her in."

We waited until Honey left the room. Actually, we all watched her leave.

"I know you know all about Sherri West being in the debut issue of my new magazine." Wyder chuckled. "Walters told me you're the ones found her and broke the news to Arnold Long." He slapped his knee and the chuckle turned into a laugh. There was something very sinister about this man's laugh.

Walters laughed along with him. He had to—he was on the payroll. I wasn't, so I merely offered a perfunctory smile. Nate was even less generous.

"You see, we got her scheduled for some publicity stuff," Wyder continued. He was talking faster now. "Like, she's going down to Indianapolis to appear at the boat show. And then Walters is going to see if we can get her some things with the media, too. But I'm kind of worried about it, you know?"

I shrugged. "What's there to worry about?"

"Well, I think she might need some protection."

"Protection from what?" Nate asked.

Wyder shrugged. "I don't know. But she was gettin' these threats from this crazy minister."

I shook my head. "I really don't think you have to worry about the Reverend Whitey Howard. We checked him out. He's not too likely to follow Sherri down to Indianapolis."

Wyder paused. It was clear he wasn't satisfied with my answer. "Well," he said, "there's always Arnold Long to think about."

"Arnold Long? What about him?"

"He just might *try* something," Wyder said, as if the answer to my question were perfectly obvious.

I didn't know whether to laugh or get mad. I just looked at Nate, who appeared to be equally mystified.

Wyder pointed a finger at us. He wore a gaudy ring on it. It was one of three on his hands, the other two forming a matched pair on his pinkies. "You guys may think you know Arnold Long, but you don't know him like I know him. He may have behaved like a perfect gentleman when you met him, but trust me: Arnold ain't no gentleman."

"Trust *me*, Len," I answered. "Long didn't behave like a gentleman. But I can tell you this for sure: He wouldn't do anything to harm Sherri West."

Wyder motioned toward his PR man. "Walters can tell you stories that would curl your toes."

I preempted Walters with a wave of my hand. "My toes have been curled plenty already," I said. "Arnold Long wouldn't lay a hand on Sherri West."

Wyder looked unconvinced. Before he could formulate another response, I added, "And we're investigators, not babysitters."

"Oh, no, I don't want you to babysit," Wyder explained. "I got Walters and my daughter, Faith, to do that. I want to hire you for security."

Nate grinned. I figured he was probably reacting to the notion of Bill Walters being the world's highest paid babysitter, but any number of things could have amused him. Consider, for example, the idea of leaving Faith Wyder alone with Sherri West.

"Len," he said, getting up from his stool. "What you need is a rent-a-cop. Check the *Yellow Pages* under Security Engineer."

I got up and stood beside him. He was already inching toward the door.

"So you mean you're turning me down?" Wyder's tone was surprise threaded with bruised feelings.

I nodded. In some ways, I was surprising myself. If Len Wyder had tried to hire me last week, I would have jumped at the opportunity. But I didn't know then what I knew now.

"Sorry, Len," I said, offering my hand. "Under the circumstances, what with our recent work for Arnold Long, I just don't think we're the guys you want."

He shook his head. "I'd pay you good dough."

"I'm sure you would. But there's not enough money in the world to get me to go to Indiana." Then, for Walters' sake, I added, "Bill says you're a helluva guy to work for."

We left Wyder beaming in the Niche, then made our way down the hall at such a quick pace that Walters had to break into a run to keep up.

"Thanks for the good word, Renzler."

"Think nothing of it," I said. "Just get us out of here."

"If it's not asking too much, Len did want me to introduce you to Faith," the PR man added.

Nate stopped in his tracks and glowered. I think Walters thought he was going to hit him. Instead, he said, "It is too much to ask, Walters. If Wyder wants to know why we didn't meet her, just tell him she was all tied up."

CHAPTER **14**

When I got back to New York I did the things I usually do after collecting a big pay check—drink, eat, sleep and pay my bills. This doesn't sound like anything special, but for some reason during those last two weeks of September, I felt like a changed man. I even tried smoking a little pot at one of Nate's artsy-fartsy parties in the Village. All it did was make me tired and dizzy, but the next morning I woke up feeling like a veteran of the counterculture.

Most of the credit for my good mood had to go to Marla, but some of it was attributable to one of the worst cases of pennant fever that ever hit New York. The Miracle Mets had overtaken the floundering Cubs to gain a berth in the newly devised pennant playoffs, and suddenly all the true-blue Yankee fans I knew had become diehard Mets boosters. My loyalties don't come that cheap, but I didn't mind hanging out in the bars to soak up the atmosphere. And I was already licking my chops over the haul I'd make betting on the Baltimore Orioles if the Mets got past Atlanta and into the World Series.

As glad as I was to be back home and away from the insanity of Eden and the Nook, I found myself watching the TV news and checking the papers for stories out of Chicago. It wasn't hard to find any. The Chicago Eight trial began on September 24—oh, yeah, I even bought a new desk calendar—and it was making headlines every day. The defendants in the case, charged with conspiracy to cross state lines to start a riot at the Democratic convention the year before, were trying to make a joke out of the trial by cussing, reading comic books and making pig noises. From what I could gather, the outbursts of Judge Julius Hoffman made one of Arnold Long's tantrums look like a moment of silent prayer.

I spoke to Marla on the phone a couple of times and learned that Arnold Long had decided to publish the photos of Sherri West—against the advice of his new legal department. She also felt obliged to say that although she liked me as a friend, she wanted to make sure I understood that we had "a physical relationship." I told her I wouldn't have it any other way and suggested she come out East as soon as possible for a purely physical weekend.

One day, when I was passing by the newsstand at Seventy-Second and Broadway, I saw Sherri West's face gazing at me from the covers of *Paradise* and *Nook*. I'm not one of those guys who can paw through the stroke books until the newsy tells you this ain't the public library, so I bought a copy of each.

For some reason, the photos of Sherri did not seem to bear much resemblance to the cute little blonde I had found in the throes of psychedelic splendor a couple of weeks before. In Arnold Long's magazine, she appeared to be about seven feet tall. On the pages of Wyder's rag, she was fuzzy and out of focus. The *Nook* spread had a headline proclaiming Sherri West "A Fallen Angel" and complete details of how Len Wyder had "snatched the snatch" right out from under Arnold Long's nose. I figured Arnold must have gone right through the roof when he saw it.

I didn't bother to rationalize my purchase by trying to read all those good articles around the pictures. I gave the magazines to Pressie, the old black doorman who sat guard in the lobby of my building. Pressie passed his days listening to jazz on a portable tape recorder between naps, and I figured they might just help him stay awake for a few hours. After that, I didn't think about *Paradise* or *Nook* or Sherri West or Arnold Long or Len Wyder again.

Until the phone call came.

It was early Monday morning, October 6. I was sleeping off a king-size hangover that I had acquired Sunday while watching the Mets and Orioles knock off the Braves and Twins for the second time in a row.

It promised to be another busy day. First there would be hair of the dog, then more baseball, then more dog. Later on, assuming the Mets and Orioles won again, it would be time to start working up a sucker list for my World Series bets.

Probably the only thing that could ruin a day as perfect as the one facing me was a death in the family. Or a call from Bill Walters.

The PR man zapped my ear with one of those taut whispers that, spoken at the right frequency, might just as well be a bloodcurdling scream. Walters hit exactly the right frequency. I don't have to tell you what it did for my headache.

"Renzler," he hissed. "You've got to come out here right away."

What do you say to that? I rolled over, lit a Marlboro and checked the Utica Club beer clock on my night table. It was six fucking A.M.

"Renzler, it's Walters. Are you there?"

"I'm here, Bill. Do you know what time it is?"

"I'm sorry, I really am. I tried to wait a bit, but Long made me call you. I know how it is. I've been up all night."

"You sound like it. What are you doing working for Long again?" I would have sounded surprised, but curiosity was all I could muster at that hour.

"I'm working for both of them. They need you out here right away. Sherri's been kidnapped."

Oh shit. My dream day was turning into a nightmare, and the sun had barely come up yet.

"Are you sure? Or did she take a hike?" I lean toward short sentences and monosyllables in the morning. Black, no sugar.

"I'm positive. They took Steve Farrell, too. I was there. It was in Indianapolis at the Holiday Inn. We were in our suite eating room service—Sherri, Steve and me. I guess it was about eleven o'clock, because we were at the boat show all day long. All of a sudden, these two guys, big guys, burst into the room, and they just grabbed her, you know?"

Walters was talking at such high speed that *my* adrenaline was flowing. I was out of bed and standing at the stove now, trying not to watch the water boil.

"They caught me right in the middle of a mouthful of my baked potato. They made Sherri and Steve line up against the wall, but I was having none of it. Farrell's standing there like a wimp, and I'm trying to fight both of them. I hit the one guy with a pretty good right hand, but the other one slugged me from behind. One guy, you know, I think I could've handled. But two guys, man . . ."

"Well, don't worry about it," I reassured him. I was drinking coffee now, and it made all the difference. "You can't fight off two guys when they surprise you like that. At least you got a good look at them. That's what counts."

"No, I didn't," he said. "They were wearing Richard Nixon masks."

I took a mouthful of coffee and suppressed a laugh. I'd have to remember that detail for Nate. It was a nice touch.

"But I got up and chased them," Walters continued. "They took off in an orange Volkswagen van. I didn't get the license number but it had Illinois plates."

"Good work, Bill." I felt like Dad talking to Junior. "Did you call the police?"

"No." He paused. "I thought of that, but Faith didn't want it to get into the papers. I didn't understand why not. From a PR perspective, it would probably sell a lot of magazines."

"It might have helped from a personal safety perspective, too," I added.

"I know," he said. "Arnold Long called the police this morning. You'll hear all about it when you get here."

It occurred to me that Walters was being a bit presumptuous, but I heard myself say "OK." I suppose I could have turned the job down, but it was good money. More than that, I felt like I owed it to Arnold Long. You tend to get those kinds of notions when you think of yourself as a professional.

Before Walters could resolve the PR dilemma of whose plane to send for us and which estate to put us up at, I made it clear that we wouldn't be staying in any tree house this time around.

"I'll make it easy for you, Bill," I said. "I want two prepaid tickets on a commercial flight. I want a big suite in a good hotel, preferably high off the street with a view of the lake. If there's a bar you can stock full of booze, all the better. And we'll meet there this afternoon—you, Wyder, Long, their sons, daughters, anyone else you can think of—at two o'clock."

"No problem," Walters said. "No problem."

CHAPTER 15

If Bill Walters ever failed in his career as a PR guy, he could easily find work as a travel agent. He handled every detail to the letter, including my request for a view of the lake. There was a minor error regarding the booze, but it wasn't his fault. I hadn't bothered to specify brands. Nate corrected the problem by pouring the Gordon's down the toilet and calling room service for Bombay or Beefeater. While he was at it, he ordered shrimp cocktails and club sandwiches.

By one o'clock that afternoon we were lounging on the top floor of the Drake Hotel, watching Baltimore knock the snot out of Minnesota on a color TV set that would have been too big to fit in my apartment. If we weren't awaiting the Longs and Wyders, I would have found it relaxing.

Walters' selection of hotels showed more discrimination than his taste in gin. If you ask me, the Drake is as swell a place as you'll ever find to stay at. But then I'm not the sort of guy people come to for vacation advice. When I travel, I look for a Howard Johnson's when my stomach starts to growl and a Holiday Inn when the sun starts to set.

The Drake sits at the north end of Michigan Avenue on what is probably the windiest corner of the Windy City. From our window we had a postcard view of the stretch of Lake Shore Drive that you always see on TV commercials. On one side, there's Oak Street

Beach; on the other, there's the Gold Coast, a row of fashionable high rises where Chicago's equivalent of blue bloods reside.

Like any old hotel, the Drake has its share of stuffiness and traditions. One of them, I learned, was for Julius Hoffman, the conspiracy trial judge, to drink himself into oblivion in the lobby bar every afternoon around five. The old judge lived at the old hotel—in one of the rooms, not just on a barstool. It was for this reason that a mob of angry hippies marched down the Gold Coast toward the Drake two nights after we got into town. This was the official start of the Days of Rage march that Moses Godley had told me about a few weeks before.

But I'm getting way ahead of myself. The Days of Rage was nothing compared with the Hour of Madness that commenced when Bill Walters, sporting a bandage the size of Rhode Island on his head, arrived at our hotel suite at two o'clock sharp, flanked by the entourage of people who could make him jump whenever they felt like saying jump—Arnold Long and son, Len Wyder and daughter.

It was a good thing I asked for the suite. I was thinking about Nate's and my comfort when I made the request, but it was clear from the expressions on the faces of the publishers and their heirs that we were going to need all the space available to us.

I didn't know if all of them had come in one car, and I didn't bother to ask. I didn't even begin to consider who got to sit in front if they had. I only marveled that Walters had managed to get them all there. If ever there was a situation that called for more than one PR man, this was it.

One thing I did note immediately, but didn't comment on: Now that I finally had a chance to get a good look, speaking quantity not quality, at Faith Wyder's face, I realized that she was the woman Arnie Long had been dining with the last night we were in Chicago. Apparently, the hatred their fathers had for each other was not transmitted genetically. But at the present moment, I had a feeling that if they sat down at a meal together, a food fight might ensue.

Anticipating ill will, Nate and I had devised a seating plan, which he directed while I mixed drinks. There were two large couches in the room, separated by a long coffee table. He put Wyder and Faith on one couch, Long and Arnie on the other. He put Walters in the easy chair we had set at the end of the table. We had flipped a coin for our own seats. I lost and got to sit on the couch next to Faith. The winner in this arrangement got to sit alongside Arnie.

Other than the requisite exchange of pleasantries welcoming us back, there was virtual silence in the room until we all got settled in our places and armed with drinks. Having the two publishers on neutral turf gave me the advantage of controlling the meeting. It was clear they weren't going to say anything until I gave them the cue. Once they got it, they responded like dogs at the track the moment they're released to chase after the rabbit.

It was a goddamn free-for-all. I've been to tag-team wrestling matches that were more orderly. If you've ever seen one, you know what happens to the referee.

"OK, who wants to go first?" I asked.

Everyone.

I had expected that, but it was worth a try just to get a reading on the situation. Here's what happened, not exactly in the order it happened.

Long called Wyder a sleazebag, and Wyder called Long a fat, pathetic, wheezing tub of lard. Long called Wyder's daughter a bulldyke, and Wyder's daughter called Long's son a limpdick. Long's son called Wyder a gangster, and Wyder called Long's son a slick-talking, spoiled Ivy League brat. (It appeared to me that Wyder had practiced his lines in advance.) They all told Bill Walters to shut up every time he opened his mouth.

I put up my arms, to no avail.

Then Nate yelled. That always works.

I paused a moment to savor the relative calm, then spoke to Walters. "Let's start with you, Bill. You were there. Tell me, briefly, what happened."

Faith interrupted before Walters could start. "I was there, too."

I gave her a look that made her wince. It was time for the speech. I stood up.

"Sherri West has been kidnapped," I said. "I assume that we all want her back, each of us for our own reasons. We can do this like adults, or we can do it like the Ding Dong school. If we do it like adults, it will be simpler, faster, and we'll find Sherri sooner. If we do it the other way, I'm going to have to stop a lot and warn you not to be bad boys and girls. OK?"

If nothing else, I managed to divert their anger. They weren't accustomed to getting that tone from hired help. After looking each other over, they all more or less nodded at me to show they understood.

Then we did it like the Ding Dong school.

We started the show-and-tell with Billy Walters. He repeated the story he had told me on the phone almost verbatim. This time, I got the added benefit of a dramatic reenaction of his struggle with the assailants in the Richard Nixon masks. The punch he had managed to land became "a vicious overhand right" in the live version, though it was plain to see from his demonstration that he couldn't have dented a toasted marshmallow. Nate was trying his best to keep his laughter silent, but the others were making no effort to suppress their boredom. I was pretty certain they had seen and heard the story several times already.

When Walters finished, I asked Faith why she hadn't wanted to call the police. Her father rose to her defense, though she was hardly under attack.

"What are you gettin' at, Renzler?"

I shrugged. "It seems like the obvious thing to do."

"I called them, Renzler," Arnold Long said.

"Shut up, no one asked you," Wyder replied.

Arnold Long pointed his cigar at his competitor. "Don't interrupt me, asshole."

"Children, children," Nate said. "Let's not all talk at once."

That silenced them for a moment. I looked at Faith Wyder.

"I didn't want it getting in the papers," she said. "I didn't want to get any bad publicity."

Arnold Long snorted. "Publicity! That's what's behind this

whole thing to begin with. It's just a cheap publicity stunt to sell magazines."

"You're a fuckin' liar," Wyder yelled. "You're the one that went to the police to try to get it in the papers. It's you that wants the publicity."

"Don't you dare scream at Dad," Arnie Long shouted, pointing a quivering finger at Wyder.

"Shut up, half-wit," Wyder answered.

Faith let out one of her cement-mixer laughs.

"Who are you calling a half-wit, *moron?*" Arnold Long demanded. He flicked his cigar ash over the table at Wyder.

Wyder responded by spitting at his competitor. He missed, but earned half credit by getting Arnold's son.

Arnie lunged over the table at Wyder, but Faith grabbed his wrist. Incredulity deadened my reflexes for a split second, and I was unable to restrain her. She stood up, pulled him across the table, crouched, turned, pivoted, and in one sudden movement, pulled him across the table, over her back and onto the floor behind the couch.

They say that leverage is the real key to this sort of maneuver, but there was no doubting this woman was one strong son of a bitch.

Nate quickly stepped in to separate them before any damage could be inflicted. I positioned myself between their fathers to ensure that their name-calling battle would not escalate into sticks and stones.

A quick check of Arnie showed no injury more serious than a severely sprained ego. I gave them a brief lecture, then we made Arnie stand in one corner and Faith stand in another.

If they moved, Nate said, he'd break their arms.

No one moved.

It's amazing to me that at least one of them didn't simply get up and leave at that point. But I suppose they were seeking direction the way a problem child who misbehaves is really looking for discipline.

From then on, things went rather smoothly.

Arnold Long said he called the Chicago police and was told the kidnapping was a matter for the Indianapolis police. They promised to investigate but suggested he contact the FBI. Since the orange Volkswagen van that Walters saw driving away had Illinois plates, there was a good possibility that Sherri West and Steve Farrell had been taken across state lines. That made it a federal case.

"What did the FBI say?" I asked.

"Those bastards," Long answered. "They said it wasn't their jurisdiction until we could prove they were taken out of the state. Even if it did come under their area of responsibility, they said it would take a few days before they could assign an agent to the case. Besides," he added sarcastically, "I think they're busy going after all these dissidents they think are trying to overthrow the government."

"Fuck the FBI and police," Wyder said. "That's what we're hirin' you for. As one of the people that's payin' your salary, I'd like to know what you're plannin' to do."

I nodded. From the little I'd dealt with him so far, I didn't especially like Len Wyder. I hoped I wouldn't have to deal with him a lot.

"First of all," I told him, "you haven't paid us a cent yet. As for a plan, I'd just as soon leave the police out of it myself. But if you had called them last night, they might have been able to find that van. You're not just talking about the possibility of bad publicity here. You're talking about two people's lives." I paused. "Unless Sherri and Farrell are pulling another fast one."

"Aw, c'mon," Wyder said. "You gotta be kiddin'." He pointed toward Walters. "Look at the lump on that man's head. These guys mean business."

I shrugged. "It's happened before. If I were you, I wouldn't be so quick to assume it couldn't happen again."

Arnold Long nodded. I could tell he was doing a slow burn thinking about how Sherri and Farrell had tricked him. But I had a feeling he just might be gloating inside a bit over the idea of Wyder getting double-crossed, too.

"I'm inclined to think you're right," I said to Wyder. "These guys probably do mean business. Which means we have to hear from them to find out exactly what kind of business they mean to do."

"So we just sit here and do nothin'?"

"Not exactly. For one thing, I'd prefer you didn't sit here." I smiled. "You're going to get a phone call or a note. Probably a note, or you would have heard from them already."

I spoke to Arnold Long. "Chances are pretty good that you'll get one, too."

He nodded. "I'm expecting it."

"The kidnappers, if they *were* kidnapped, probably know that you're both wealthy men," I said. "That means their ransom price is going to be pretty steep."

"I'll pay anything," Arnold Long said.

"So will I," Wyder added. He paused. "As long as we're sure of gettin' the money back."

"You're *not*." I glared at him. "This is a ransom payment we're talking about, not a short-term loan."

"Cheapskate," Long muttered.

"Fuck you," Wyder replied.

"Chil*dren*!" Nate bellowed from across the room, where he was standing between Arnie and Faith. The publishers looked at him, then at each other, then at the floor.

"You're going to have to decide if you're willing to pay and how much you're willing to pay," I said. "My guess is it's going to cost you at least a quarter of a million dollars."

"*Jesus* Christ."

"That's minimum," I reminded Wyder.

"Money's no problem," Arnold said. I had a feeling he wouldn't have been so forthcoming if his competitor hadn't been there bitching and moaning.

"Good. I suggest you start getting some funds together. They're going to want cash."

"Can't we mark the bills or something?" It was clear Wyder had watched his share of bad TV cop shows.

"Sure, if you want," I answered. "You can work that out with your banker."

"You sure there's nothin' we can't do?" Wyder said. "You see, I'm a doer, not a guy who just sits around. What about that crazy preacher?"

I nodded. "We'll check him out. We'll also contact the authorities in Indiana and Illinois to see if we can get a line on that van. We'll try to find Pablo Johnson. But chances are you're going to hear from the kidnappers before we get anything to work with."

I was trying to think of a closing comment when the phone rang. Wyder almost jumped right out of his alligator shoes when he heard it. I was a bit startled myself.

Being the closest, Walters was all over the phone like the cheap suit he was wearing. But he was a model of professional deportment when he answered, saying, "Mark Renzler's suite, Bill Walters speaking."

We all watched Walters listen for a moment. Then he spoke to Arnold Long. "It's Wanda from your office. She says it's very important."

"Arnie, you take it," Long said, although he was within an arm's reach of the phone. I've always admired a man who knows how to delegate responsibility.

Arnie looked to Nate, who nodded, before he stepped away from his corner and came across the room to take the phone from Walters. The conversation was brief, with Arnie's contribution comprising only a few short questions.

He put down the phone slowly and let out a long dramatic sigh before speaking. "The police called," he said. "They've found Steve Farrell."

"Where?" his father demanded.

"Near the interstate south of Joliet. A farmer found him wandering in his cornfield."

"Where is he now?" Wyder asked.

Arnie gave the *Nook* publisher a disapproving glance, as if to indicate that Wyder had interrupted a private conversation between him and his father. He looked at Arnold. "They took him to the hospital. They want us to notify his family. They want someone to go down there and see him."

"Well, it looks like we've got something to do." I was speaking to Nate, but I said it for Wyder's benefit.

"They said he's in bad shape," Arnie cautioned. "They said he's high on drugs. He told them he was picked up by a UFO."

CHAPTER 16

By the time we got rid of the Hatfields and McCoys, it was pushing five o'clock. I was sure that God must have invented Happy Hour for days like the one we had just been through, so we headed straight for the lobby bar to offer a few up. It was there that we saw Judge Hoffman counting pinko elephants.

I filled Nate in on my discovery that Arnie Long and Faith Wyder liked eating with each other when they weren't beating on each other.

"Sounds like more than your typical love/hate relationship," he said. "Do you think they've got something cooking, like maybe a plan to burn their dear old dads?"

"I don't know. I doubt it. But just in case, I think we should wait until just the right moment before bringing it up."

When we got back to the suite, I went through the formality of calling the state police in Indiana and Illinois. I got just the response I expected. They would notify troopers to keep an eye open for the van. This is as much as you can ask for from people who are in the habit of working with both eyes closed.

The Illinois cop I spoke to, a Sergeant Michaels, pointed out that one out of every three longhairs was driving a Volkswagen van these days.

"But it's orange," I told him. "At least that gives you a little more to go on."

"That's the most popular color," he replied.

I wished him luck in finishing out the rest of his years before early retirement, then got down to the important business at hand—showering and shaving before Marla and Mindi came over.

It turned out that the girls liked baseball—or at least they said they did—so I got to have my cake and eat it, too, after all. The Mets kicked Atlanta's ass one last time before moving on to the World Series against Baltimore. I figured I was missing out on a great celebration back at McCabe's, but Marla's company more than made up for the loss. Besides, I'd be the one celebrating in a week or so when I collected on my sucker bets.

Around noon the next day, we set out for St. Jude's Hospital in Normal, Illinois, to see Steve Farrell. Normally, I don't let clients accompany me on assignments, but this time I made an exception and allowed Bill Walters to come along. I figured it would be a good idea to have someone who knew Farrell with us when we tried to talk to him. From the thumbnail sketch we'd gotten on his condition, I had a feeling he wasn't going to have anything of much value to tell us.

Of course, nothing was simple. Len Wyder wanted us to take Faith, and Long wanted us to take Arnie. I explained that there wouldn't be enough room in the car once we set up the kiddie seats. After a bit of three-way phone haggling that took up most of the morning, we compromised on Walters. If I had to check out every move I made with Long and Wyder, we were never going to find Sherri.

Normal, it turned out, was a lot farther south of Joliet than I had been led to believe. It was a three-hour ride that felt like six, because you had to cross the sprawling southwest side of Chicago to get there. This area is a wasteland of such dimension that it rivals the strip of the New Jersey Turnpike between Newark and New York for world-class scenic affronts.

It was probably just a coincidence that Steve Farrell was taken to a hospital called St. Jude's. But I suppose there's always the outside chance that the cop who picked him up had a sense of humor. If you're not familiar with the Catholic registry of VIPs, you might not know that Jude is the patron saint of lost causes.

It's a lousy name for a hospital, I'll grant you. But there was no doubt Steve Farrell ended up in the right place.

Before going to see him, we were taken to the office of a Dr. Howard Hardiman, the headshrinker in residence. After doing the introductions, Walters told Hardiman that Farrell's parents had been contacted and would be flying in from Topeka later that day.

"Mr. Farrell has taken a massive dose of lysergic acid diethylamide," Hardiman said. He tilted his head to the side when he talked.

"LSD," Nate said.

"Yes, that's right." Hardiman gave us a smile that made me wonder if he had ever indulged in psychedelics himself. Then he tilted his head into speaking position and launched into an eloquent but nonetheless incomprehensible explanation of Steve Farrell's condition. He noted that the photographer was suffering severe neurovascular spasmodic episodes—or was it episodic spasms?—resulting in a delusional psychosis of what would appear to be irrevocable consequence. When Walters told him about the kidnapping, he said that a cathartic event such as that, given its temporal proximity, would only amplify the traumatization.

In other words, Steve Farrell was a fucking vegetable.

I told Hardiman that Farrell liked to take drugs. I wondered if the LSD he had taken was a self-administered dose.

Double tilt. "It's highly unlikely that anyone would take that massive a dose for recreational purposes," he said.

I asked him how much LSD he thought Farrell had taken.

"That's very difficult to ascertain, but my conjecture would be approximately 2,500 micrograms."

I nodded, pretending to do a calculation.

"Figure about five or six hits," Nate explained.

"Yes, that's right." Hardiman was giving us that smile again.

"I sure feel lucky to know someone who's in with the in-crowd," I told Nate. "But aren't you a little old for that sort of thing."

He folded his arms and assumed his Zen Buddhist tone of voice. "Age is merely a state of mind, grasshopper."

Hardiman took us to the elevator and up to Farrell's room.

Because of the stories I had heard about people on LSD thinking they could fly, I thought it was a little strange to put someone in his condition on the fourth floor. Then I saw the gates on the windows.

Then I saw Steve Farrell. This guy wasn't going anywhere.

Moses Godley had said Pablo Johnson thought it would be a great idea to spike the Chicago water supply with LSD. If Steve Farrell's condition was even a remote indication of what it might do to people, Pablo was one fucking deranged son of a bitch.

Farrell was propped up on a bed, his arms hanging motionless at his sides. His eyes were wide open, but they looked so empty they might just as well have been closed. It was hard to say that he was actually staring, but he was—into space.

"You can talk to him," Hardiman said. "But I wouldn't be surprised if he doesn't recognize you."

No shit, Doc.

Being the guy with the professional social skills, Walters moved in closer to make the first swoop. "Steve, it's me," he said. "Bill Walters. You know, the PR director from *Paradise*. I mean, I work for *Nook* now. You know, we both do."

It was obviously no go, but that didn't stop Walters from trying some more.

"Remember the time we went to New York together for the magazine convention? Remember we were at that party and that big black guy cornered us? He must have been seven feet tall. And every time one of us said something, he'd say, 'Ah know what *time* it is'?"

Walters punched the photographer softly on the shoulder. "Come on, Steve," he urged. "You remember. You've got to remember."

There was no response at first, then Farrell began to cry. Then, at last, he began to talk. I don't do it justice by saying it was probably the spookiest voice I've ever heard.

"You hurt me," he said to Walters, still staring straight ahead. "Get away from me. You hurt me."

Walters looked at us. His expression was wild. I couldn't blame him. If you didn't know Farrell was helpless, he would have scared the shit out of you.

"Don't worry," Hardiman assured him. "You didn't hurt him. He's not feeling any pain."

Easy for you to say, Doc.

Walters nodded. "Maybe you should give it a try," he said to me.

I walked around to the foot of the bed, so that I was standing directly in Farrell's line of vision. Which is to say I was standing right where his eyes were staring.

I decided to try a more recent memory. "Farrell, I was at your apartment a couple of weeks ago. You were there with Sherri. You were both high on mescaline."

It might have been my imagination, but I thought the photographer smiled slightly at the reference to his favorite drug.

"Can I yell at him?" I asked Hardiman.

He tilted and shrugged. "I don't see why not. It might even help him to hear you."

"You dumb fucking asshole," I shouted. Hardiman didn't look entirely pleased with my choice of words. "What happened the night before last? You were in Indianapolis. You and Sherri. Two men took you away in a Volkswagen van. Do you remember that?"

Evidently, he didn't.

"Pablo Johnson," I shouted. "Pablo. Does that mean anything to you?"

No sirree, it sure did not. But after a few more shouts, Farrell did start to talk.

"It was the Martians." He was speaking in a different voice this time, like that of a nursery school teacher telling a fairy tale to little Johnny. If he had been singing instead of talking, the melody would have been "Twinkle, Twinkle, Little Star."

"They came down in their spaceship. They asked me to show them the way to the next whiskey bar. We went for a long, long, long, long ride. We went to Pluto and Jupiter and Neptune. Then we went to the Mars bar and had a Milky Way."

Farrell was grinning now. I don't need to tell you that it was a vacant grin.

He pointed to Walters. "You were there, Frodo." Then to Nate. "And you, too, Bilbo." The talking stopped, but the grin remained.

"Jesus Christ," Walters said.

"Yeah, he was probably in the spaceship with him, too," Nate answered.

The humor was lost on Hardiman. "He's been talking like that on and off since he got here," the doctor explained. "He hums, too."

"He seems to be stringing his words together well," I said. "The thoughts are incoherent, but the diction's OK. Does that mean there's a better chance he'll recover?"

Hardiman tilted. "Total recovery? Unlikely, I think. But that's extremely difficult to say right now. We'll only be able to gauge that after we ascertain the quantity of brain damage that he has sustained."

"I see." I looked at Nate. "What do you think?"

"I think this poor slob doesn't have a shot in hell at getting back to Kansas."

I nodded. "I think I don't want to be here when his mother arrives."

CHAPTER 17

Wednesday, October 8, 1969, was probably the longest day of my entire life. It started, like most of my bad days do, with an early morning phone call.

This time, it wasn't Bill Walters. It was Arnie Long.

"It came," he said in a terse, dramatic voice.

"What did?" I asked, matching him in terseness, minus the drama.

"The ransom note."

"When?" I lit a cigarette and watched Nate roll out of bed across the suite and call room service for coffee on the other phone.

"Last night. I don't know when exactly. It was inside the door this morning."

"That's close enough. Was it sent by mail or delivered by hand?"

"Well, there was no postmark on the envelope."

"That means it was delivered by hand." I guess I had it out for young Arnie in a way.

"You were right. They want two hundred and fifty thousand." Bingo. I hoped my prediction of Baltimore winning the Series would be that close to target.

"And guess what?"

I don't like to guess. After a long pause, I guess he figured that out.

"It's written on People Against Pornography paper," he said.

"That figures. Was it written or typed?"

"Printed."

"OK. What does it say?"

He began to summarize. I stopped him and told him to read it to me word for word.

"It's pretty long," he cautioned.

"I've got time if you do." If we had been speaking face to face, I would have looked at my watch for effect.

"To Arnold Long. Sherri West is alive and well. You can get her back. Here's how. It will cost you $250,000 in cash. No checks or credit cards please. On Thursday at noon, Faith Wyder should carry the money inside a large plain brown envelope in a suitcase to the northeast corner outside the bird house at the Lincoln Park Zoo (see map enclosed). She should also carry the money from Len Wyder. He is getting the same note. She should come alone. No one should follow her. The Lord will punish those who disobey.

"In the designated spot on the map, she will find a suitcase behind the elm tree. She should put the envelope from you and the envelope from Len Wyder inside the suitcase and take the note out of it. The note will have full instructions on where you can find Sherri West.

"Sherri has great tits. If you do not exactly follow the instructions to the letter, she will get one of them cut off. So do not let your detective go snooping around. The Lord sees all. He is all-merciful. He is all-knowing. May he forgive you for your sins. If it were up to me, I would not."

I could tell by Arnie's pause that he had reached the end. "I think there are some clues in here, don't you?" he asked.

"What are they?" When I'm in the right mood, I enjoy watching my clients play detective. I was getting in the right mood now. The coffee had arrived.

"All this Christian nonsense. Do you think Reverend Whitey's behind it, after all?"

"Highly unlikely," I said. I couldn't see any point in trying to explain what a frame job is. Especially since this was such a bad one. "We'll have time to pay him a visit today, anyway. He has some explaining to do about who has access to his stationery." I didn't mention that I was positive he must know Pablo Johnson.

"Well, it sounds like we could just wait for him at the drop-off site, doesn't it?"

"Uh, no, Arnie. It's not that simple. There were two men who broke into the hotel room that night. Unless they've planned this very badly—and it sounds like they haven't—one of them will be posted near the drop site. If he sees one of us there, they'll call it off and make us do it over again. In return for our failure to cooperate, they just might hurt Sherri."

"Hmm." The wheels in Arnie's head were spinning so fast, I could feel a headache coming on. "Well, what do we do?"

"Basically, we follow the instructions. I assume your father's willing to pay the money."

"Are you kidding?" Arnie sounded slightly insulted. "Dad would pay anything to get Sherri back."

"That's what I thought."

"So you mean we're just going to *give* our money away?"

I didn't bother to remind Arnie that it was "Dad's" money we were talking about giving away. "One of us will follow Faith," I said.

"But the letter says not to."

I was losing my patience again. It must have been a soft year for Ivy League admissions when Arnie graduated from high school. Or maybe he knew someone. That's right—his father! My brain wasn't exactly on full throttle yet.

"Do you have a better idea?" I asked.

"No." Bruised ego again. "But it's going to be very difficult to follow her tomorrow. The park is where all the anti-war demonstrators are going to assemble."

"I know." I read the papers, too, kid. Even if I do spend half an hour on the sports and five minutes on the news section. "I told you they've planned it pretty well."

"I see." Pregnant pause. "Then there's nothing we can do."

"I didn't say that. Nate and I will talk it over. We'll check out the drop site. We'll think of something. At the very least, we should get Sherri back, and that's what your father wants. How's he holding up, by the way?"

"I guess he's OK. He's been in an exceptionally bad mood."

"I'm not surprised. That can be your job—keeping his spirits up." Christ, did I really say that? I was talking to him as if he were nine instead of twenty-nine.

"How's Steve Farrell?" he asked. "Did he tell you anything?"

"No. He's in bad shape. It was like talking to a piece of broccoli. You work on getting the money together. I'll call you later in the day."

"I'll be waiting."

I filled Nate in as soon as I got off the phone. We began to talk over the most significant element of the letter from my standpoint—the clue that Arnie Long had failed to notice.

The letter made reference to "your detective." Evidently, Pablo Johnson, or whoever wrote it, had spoken to someone Nate or I had talked to.

But who? Someone from *Paradise* or *Nook*? Reverend Whitey?

Our conversation didn't get very far. I knew it wouldn't. We were due for another phone call.

"Renzler. It came. Whadda we do now?"

I was tempted to tell Len Wyder that here on land you didn't have to shout, that telephones had built-in amplifiers to save you that trouble. But I refrained. After all, he was a man who stood to loose $250,000.

"I know," I said.

"Whaddaya mean, you know?"

"Arnie Long called. He read me the note his father received."

"Hmm. Is that so?" Wyder paused. I had a sense that his feelings were hurt because he was not the first one to get a letter. I didn't risk adding to his sense of insecurity by suggesting it might just be a case of his sleeping later than the competition.

"Well," he shouted. "Lemme read you mine. It might be different. There might be a new clue in it for you."

It wasn't. There wasn't. But I listened to the whole thing again, just in case I had missed something the first time around. I hadn't.

When Wyder finished reading, we had pretty much the same conversation I had with Arnie Long. The only real difference was that I was a bit more patient with Wyder, because it was his money and he had taken the time to call himself.

He, too, thought that we should set up a stake-out and suspected that Reverend Whitey was our man. Like Arnie, he failed to notice the clue. And, he wanted my assurance that, whatever happened, his "baby" would not get hurt.

"Don't worry about Faith. She'll be as safe as if she were home in bed," I promised. The humor was wasted on Wyder, but I could see Nate laughing across the room.

The only time I got short with Wyder was when he pressed me about the letter Arnold Long had received.

"How much does that cheap kike have to pay?" he demanded.

"Do you mean Mr. Long?"

"Yeah, that's who I mean."

"Mr. Long has to pay 250 Gs, just like you."

"Are you sure they're not lettin' him off easy and you're not just sayin' that?"

"I'm goddamn positive," I retorted. "And if I was just saying it, I'd still be saying it now, wouldn't I?" In the back of my mind, I was just about certain Len Wyder was going to stiff me on my bill. Which was just fine. There are ways to deal with that.

"What about the bills? Should I mark 'em?"

"That's an area where they slipped up," I told him. "They didn't specify. If I were you, I'd give them the biggest bills you can get. That way, they'll be easier to trace."

"Yeah, that makes good sense."

Thanks for the endorsement. I told him we'd all meet at Eden at 11 A.M. Thursday.

"Why do I gotta go to *his* place?"

I started to load both barrels. He must have felt it coming, because he changed gears before I could fire. "I mean, we could have a great brunch over at my place."

I ignored the invitation. "Long's house is closer to the park. We'll leave from there. Call me here if you have any more questions."

I left it at that, and left him hanging at the other end. Room service arrived with eggs Benedict that Nate had ordered, and there's nothing I hate more than cold eggs.

Except perhaps lousy clients. Followed by cold eggs.

CHAPTER 18

By the time we finished chowing down and showering up, our rental car was waiting downstairs. Bill Walters had called and offered to chauffeur us around in his Cadillac, but I turned him down. As I said, I was getting to like the guy in a funny sort of way. But I didn't want him to think we were going steady or anything.

Besides, our rental car was a Mercedes.

The first business of the day was to scope out the area around the drop site. I wanted to get our bearings down exactly in case we lost Faith Wyder in the crowd the following day. I had no idea just how many longhairs would turn out for the demonstration, but from the media reports, it sounded as if they were expecting thousands. After the fiasco at the '68 Democratic convention, you could be sure Mayor Daley would send out at least that many cops.

Some of the protestors were already beginning to straggle in, so it took us a while to get through the traffic on the road through Lincoln Park. Once we got to the zoo, it didn't take long to find the bird house. It was at the far north corner on the side near the lake.

The kidnappers had picked a smart spot for the drop. Right behind the northeast corner of the bird house was a path leading to a long parking lot that ran from Fullerton Parkway down to North Avenue. Both Fullerton and North emptied right out onto Lake Shore Drive. Once someone picked up the money, he could either get into a car in the lot or walk about fifty yards up to Fullerton.

There was no suitcase at the spot yet, but the elm tree was right there waiting for it. I had hoped the tree would be suitable for climbing and big enough to hide in. It wasn't. It was a dead elm tree. There were no others nearby.

So it goes. I didn't much relish the idea of spending a night in a tree, anyway. But unless we stayed very close to Faith Wyder, it was going to be tough to stop the person who was picking up the money.

We got back in the car and found our way over to Ogden Avenue, a neglected diagonal that starts near a row of housing projects on the North Side and runs past a row of housing projects on the West Side to a row of housing projects on the South Side. It's one of the many parts of Chicago they don't tell you about at the tourism office.

It was time to pay a visit to the Reverend Whitey Howard. We didn't need any spiritual counseling, but we thought he could probably use a little friendly persuasion.

It turned out he needed a lot more than that.

We turned west when we hit Madison Street, just before the intersection of Ashland Avenue. Or, I should say, we tried to turn. There was a sizable traffic jam, but it didn't have anything to do with commuters. It wasn't rush hour by a long shot, and they don't travel this part of town, anyway.

A crowd of hippies was spilling onto Madison outside a dilapidated storefront. After getting out of the car, we found out that it was the local headquarters for SDS. A line of cops was trying to get the hippies to move back off the street. But the hippies weren't demonstrating, and the cops weren't watching them. *They* were watching the cops. Or at least that's what it looked like to us until we pulled over and got out of the car.

"We can walk from here," Nate said. "Reverend Whitey's place is about two blocks over on Madison."

It wasn't necessary to go that far to see him. For some reason, Reverend Whitey Howard had decided to set up shop in the center of the intersection that day. So eager was he to get out and preach that he had forgotten to put on any clothes.

He was surrounded by police, but they weren't there to hear his sermon. They couldn't have understood him, anyway. He was speaking in another language, one that I sure as hell didn't recognize. Tongues, maybe.

I'm certain the cops would have stepped in to grab him if he hadn't been swinging a four-foot crucifix for emphasis. For the time being, they were trying to reason with him.

Good luck.

"It's like he's on acid or something," I heard a frizzy-haired girl in a print dress say, as we walked by the SDS store. "The guy's totally freaking out."

"I know," a bearded man beside her answered. "It's just like a guy I saw at the Dead concert in Philly."

"In case you haven't figured it out, that's Reverend Whitey," Nate told me.

"Thanks for the tip. It looks as if Pablo Johnson has already paid him a visit."

"Indeed it does. Should we continue on to his house of worship?"

"Yeah. Let's hope we get there before the cops do."

We did. But we were afraid they might be coming any minute, so we got in and out fast. It's hard to conduct a thorough search when you're pressed for time. It's even harder when you don't know what it is you're searching for. As it happened, we made out pretty well.

Nate found it, on the bottom of a pile of papers in an old chest.

"Birth certificate," he announced. "Paul John Howard. Born in Joliet, Illinois, on the fourth of July, nineteen hundred and thirty-nine. In the year of our Lord."

"Naturally."

"I'd say it fits, wouldn't you? Paul Howard. Howard Johnson. Paul Johnson."

"Almost like a glove. The kid must be a fan of the twenty-eight flavors. We know who Pop is. What about Mom? If we can locate her, we might be able to find Pablo."

Nate sifted through a few more papers, then held up another document. "Death certificate," he said. "Alice Johnson Howard. Nineteen fifty-four."

"Now it really fits," I said. "How'd she die?"

"Yeah, like a dirty sock. Ruling of suicide."

"Overdose of fried clams?"

"It doesn't say."

"Based on what we know about her son and husband, I can't say that I blame her."

"Amen."

By the time we got back to the intersection, the police had restrained Whitey Howard and were putting him into an ambulance. After our conversation with Steve Farrell the day before, I couldn't see any point in trying to talk to him. But I was damn curious why his son had stuffed him full of drugs. He must have known something that Pablo didn't want him telling us. Or maybe Nate's visit had upset him and he had questioned Pablo about the notes to Sherri. Or maybe . . .

There was no point in speculating. We'd probably never know the answer, unless we got Pablo to confess. To do that, we had to find him first. On a hunch, we went into the SDS store.

There were about twelve of them clustered inside. All hippies, all white, mostly guys, a few girls. No cops that I could see, unless the plain clothes division had gotten very sophisticated in recent years. They were all jabbering and laughing about Whitcy's outdoor service when we entered. But our appearance turned out to be a real conversation stopper.

I instinctively loosened my tie before speaking. There was no trouble getting their undivided attention. "Does anyone here know Pablo Johnson?"

Silence was the only answer I got. I repeated the question.

This time, a kid with a pony tail answered from behind a counter with leaflets stacked on it. "Who are you—*asshole?*"

I gave him a look that could kill, and he backed up a step. A murmur of support for him went up around me in the form of whispers. "Pig, narc." The usual stuff.

I stepped forward and put my business card with the phone

number of the Drake down on the counter in front of him. "Private investigator—*Mary Alice*."

More murmurs went up, and Nate began to eye the crowd. I did a quick once-over for my own benefit.

There were eight males altogether. None of them looked like they had been star linebackers on their high school football teams. I've got nothing against Women's Lib, but I didn't bother to count the girls.

Nate was moving ever so slowly in a circle, sizing up the group. He made a wider arc each time he turned, and they were backing up against the walls to make room for him. When he wanted to, Nate could look very mean. He looked like he wanted to. The longer the hippies looked at him looking at them like that, the more cooperative they were likely to be.

He came to a stop, looked at me and grinned. "Piece of cake," he said.

I repeated my question: "Does anyone here know Pablo Johnson?"

"Why are you asking?" It was a girl who spoke up, the frizzy-haired girl I had seen outside.

"That was his old man out there," I said.

"What?" The gasps started slowly, then became a chorus.

"How do you know?" another kid asked me.

"I just know, that's all." I paused to let it sink in that we were there to ask questions, not answer them. "When's the last time you saw him?" I asked the room.

"He was here this morning." The girl again.

"Does anyone here know where he lives?"

No answer.

I let my eyes circle the room.

A tall, skinny kid with glasses near the door spoke up. "He was living with that chick from *Paradise* magazine, wasn't he?"

"Hey, don't tell this guy anything." The kid from behind the counter was talking again.

"Ah, who cares? Pablo's a jerk-off," a kid in the corner said.

"You're right," I said. "And he's in deep shit this time. *Real* deep shit."

I waited for volunteers, but there weren't any. Finally, the girl spoke up again. "Listen, mister, we don't know where he lives. None of us like him very much. OK?"

Her statement sounded like a plea for us to leave. We accepted it.

I could feel them staring at us as we walked toward the door. When we reached it, Nate turned and raised his fist in the air. "Off the pigs," he said. "Bring the war home."

A cheer went up in the room.

"You really have a way with this younger generation," I told him as we got into the car.

He shrugged. "It's nothing. You just have to understand where they're *coming* from, man. You'll catch on—after your first acid trip."

"I hear you. I hear you."

CHAPTER 19

It was pushing three o'clock by the time we got back to the Drake. I had flirted with the idea of stopping by Eden to confer with Arnold Long in person, but my better judgment and a stern protest from Nate got the best of me. The temptation to go there probably had more to do with my desire to see Marla than it did my sense of professional responsibility. But I had a date with the former and a telephone to take care of the latter.

Judging by our stack of messages, the telephone had been busier than we were. Marla and Mindi had each called, probably to confirm our double date rendezvous for the evening. Kathy O'Leary had phoned long distance—did I forget to send her check? Bill Walters called twice, urgent on each occasion. Arnie Long went one further with three urgents.

We took care of pleasure before business, arranging for dinner at the Berghoff, a swell restaurant in the Loop. I dodged the ex entirely. Bill Walters, it turned out, had left the Nook for the day. Strange behavior, I thought, given the situation. But nothing surprised me on this case. The secretary, who had a voice like Minnie Mouse, was not at liberty to give out his home phone number. Fine with me. No, I didn't want to talk to Mr. Wyder or his daughter. If Walters wanted to talk to me, he had my number. Boy, did he ever.

No such luck with Arnie Long. From the irritation in his voice,

I gathered that he had been glued to his desk waiting to hear from me.

"You said you were going to call later."

"This is later."

"I called you three times."

"I know."

"Why didn't you call me back?"

"I am calling you back."

"Where were you?"

At a whorehouse, Junior. "We were out. Working."

"What happened with the Reverend Whitey Howard? I thought you were going to keep me posted."

Indeed. It was probably a good thing we hadn't gone to Eden. If Arnie had carried on like this in person, I'd probably be facing fifty years for manslaughter. Or maybe life for murder one.

Luckily, Nate handed me a beer. That always has a calming influence. At least the first one does, anyway.

But as I bristled under Arnie Long's supervisory tone, I began to wonder if there was something more than officious curiosity at work. Based on the slip-up in the ransom note, I was pretty sure that someone on the inside had told the kidnappers about me. I didn't think Arnie would plot to steal money from his own father, but like I said, nothing on this case would surprise me. And though I hadn't thought much about it, I was still curious what Arnie and Faith Wyder had been talking about the evening I saw them dining together.

I make it a policy to trust my clients. But I also make it a policy only to tell them as much or as little as I think they need to know. There wasn't very much I was going to tell Arnie Long.

"I think your hunch about old Reverend Whitey was wrong, Arnie."

"What do you mean? Did you talk to him?"

"Nope. No need to. Someone administered the same sacrament to Whitey that Steve Farrell received."

"Another drug overdose?" If Arnie was pretending to be surprised, he was a very good actor.

"That's right. Another candidate for the broccoli patch. The police carted him away."

"Do they have any idea who did it?"

"I didn't talk to them, Arnie. I've got my own idea."

I listened to him wait, then waited for him to ask.

"Pablo Johnson," I said. "That's my guess." I didn't tell him it was more than just a guess.

The beer was nearing empty, so I changed the subject. "Have you got the money together?"

"Yes, that's all arranged. I've had a very busy day."

Tell me about it. "I told Len Wyder we'd meet at your place at eleven o'clock tomorrow morning. Is that OK with you?" I thought it damn well better be.

"Well, yes, I suppose so. That makes sense, doesn't it?"

No, it doesn't. That's why I suggested it.

Nate was standing in front of me gazing at his watch. "I'll see you then," I said. I hung up before he could think of any more questions.

"I think maybe that kid took too many drugs in college," I said.

Nate shook his head. "I think it's a case of not enough."

If I had known then how the evening was going to go, I would have crawled under the covers and told the desk to hold my calls. Since I didn't, we ventured downstairs to the bar to watch the Julius Hoffman show.

Based on the radio report we had heard in the car, it sounded like the old codger had been through one hell of a day in court. With hippies marching into town from all over the country, there was no telling what kind of fallout the judge would start radiating once he pumped a few down.

Our entertainment turned out to be short-lived. If there's a Bill, there's a way, and Walters managed to find it. We were working on our second round when he paged me.

"I figured you'd be in the bar," he said. He was trying to sound lighthearted, but I could tell from the wavering in his voice that he hadn't called just to chat.

"Yeah, we ran out of booze in the suite."

He chuckled. It was a forced chuckle.

"I tried you at your office," I said, "but the secretary told me you left for the day. Are you sick?"

"I don't know. I guess you could say that. I don't know. I had some thinking to do."

"It sounds like it. You don't know whether or not you're sick? It sounds to me like you need a drink."

"Yes, I do. I probably do. I've got something to tell you. It's important."

"Sure, go right ahead."

"No, I don't want to talk to you on the phone."

"OK. Tell me where and when." I was hoping he'd make it close and quick.

"It's more complicated than that."

"How complicated is it, Bill?" I was thinking maybe I should finish college and become a therapist. They make better money and they have better hours. Plus, I think they deal with a saner bunch of people than I do.

"Very complicated."

"I see." A friend of mine who's a therapist told me she always says "I see" when she doesn't know what to say.

"It's going to cost you."

"What?" I flagged down a waiter and signaled for a refill. "I see."

"I don't mean it's going to cost you. I mean it's going to cost Arnold Long. And Wyder, too."

"How much?"

"Twenty-five thousand dollars."

"You've got to be out of your fucking mind!"

Bad timing. The waiter came with my drink and my check right when I hit the crescendo. I apologized with my hands and pulled a buck out of my pocket for his trouble.

"I know it sounds crazy, but it isn't." Walters was talking with more confidence in his voice now. "Believe me, Renzler. Those two guys have money to burn. I know for a fact that Long keeps a hundred thousand stashed in a safe in the Sanctuary. And Wyder's got plenty of cash around. And they'd be splitting it, so it's only twelve-five apiece."

"You're missing the point, Walters. What makes you think they'd pay that much money to *you*?"

"Because of what they'll save. I'm only charging them each five percent of the ransom."

Right. Sounds perfectly logical to me. "And what is it that you have to sell?"

"Oh, no. If I told you that, then I wouldn't get paid for it."

Ah, yes. You have to get up pretty early in the morning to fool Bill Walters.

"Listen, moron," I said. "You have to at least give me some idea."

I downed half my drink while he deliberated.

"Well, all right," he said. "I know it all. Or at least I know a lot of it. I can tell you all about what really happened that night in Indianapolis."

"You were in on it," I said.

"Well, not exactly."

"They paid you off to tell your silly story and keep your mouth shut," I said. "And then, when the ransom note came and you saw how much they were asking, you felt like they stiffed you."

"Exactly."

"How much did they pay you?"

"Well . . ."

"Go ahead, you can tell me."

"Ten thousand." I could almost feel his face turning red over the phone.

"You got stiffed," I said.

"You're telling me." He sounded like a kid who had just traded away a Roger Maris for a Roger Repoz.

"OK, I'll see what I can do. It's going to take a little while to convince Long and Wyder to pay you off."

"Don't worry. I know you can do it."

Thanks, Bill. It's people like you having confidence in me that makes the job so rewarding. I looked at my watch. Damn. It was going to be a late dinner. "How about seven o'clock? If they don't come up with the money, I'll call you."

"No problem." He let out a sigh of relief that would have made an elephant fart seem trifling by comparison. "You know, Renzler, I really feel better now that I talked to you."

Yeah, don't mention it. "Where do we meet you?"

"How about the Paradise Room?"

"Are you kidding?" Somehow, that sounded to me like knocking off your old man and then playing nine holes with his clubs.

"Why not? I've still got a charge account there." He let out a laugh.

"There's just one hitch that you might want to think about, Walters."

The laughing stopped. "What's that?"

"After you give us the info, what's to stop us from strangling you?"

I hung up before he could formulate an answer.

CHAPTER 20

We had one for the road while we planned a course of action. I had no desire to talk to Arnie Long on the phone again. I had even less desire to see him in person. Then there was the matter of Len Wyder. Getting money out of him would be harder than growing roses on Astroturf.

I just might wind up strangling Bill Walters after all.

But in a strange sort of way, I felt good about his phone call. It wasn't my money, after all, and it was the first solid break we had gotten so far. It was about time.

I went upstairs to our suite to make the calls while Nate went around the corner to get the car. This is the price I get to pay for being the detective instead of the leg man. I would have given both my legs to trade assignments with him.

If Arnie Long thought I was terse in our previous phone conversations, he probably thought I was downright rude this time. I wasn't. I was just cryptic. I told him that something very important had come up, that Nate and I would be there to meet with his father—I didn't bother to invite him—in half an hour. I told him that he should have 12,500 bucks ready for me when we got there. If he had any questions, he could ask us then.

He started to say something about Dad having an important party. Without saying it, I implied it would be in Dad's best interest to cancel it—I hung up on him.

When I called the Nook, I got Minnie Mouse again. I asked for Len Wyder.

"Mr. Wyder can't be disturbed," she squeaked.

"This is urgent," I said. I think I might have raised my voice a bit.

"I'm very sorry. He's in a session."

I could have asked what that meant, but I had a feeling I didn't want to know.

"What about Faith?" I asked. "Is she in a session, too?"

"Oh, no." She was practically squealing now. It was as if someone pinched her ass automatically when she answered the phone. "Not on Wednesday night."

Oh, that's right. She bowls on Wednesday, doesn't she?

"Put her on the line," I said. "Tell her it's Mark Renzler, and tell her it's urgent."

"Oh, hello, is that you, Mr. Renzler?" No, lady, it's the guy that always calls and says it's me. "Did you get hold of Mr. Walters like you wanted to?"

"Yeah, I got hold of him, but not like I wanted." Not yet, at least.

She got a good laugh—Christ, what a laugh—out of that. But I'm sure she had no idea what I was talking about. She put me on hold and put a halt to her falsetto squeaks. After a few moments of merciful silence, I was greeted by the familiar grinding of Faith Wyder's cement-mixer baritones. It was a remarkable contrast, but I wouldn't say it was an improvement.

"Hello, Renzler. How can I help you?"

Why was it that every question she asked sounded like an invitation to tango?

"I've got a problem," I said. "A big problem. Though it might turn out to be the break we need. I tried to call your father, but the secretary said he was in a session."

"That's right. He always has a love session on Wednesday."

"I see." A love session. Please, spare me the details.

"Bill Walters called me," I said hurriedly, before she could elaborate on her father's habits. "He says he wasn't telling the truth about Indianapolis. He says he has information about the kidnapping that he wants to sell."

"Why, that little weasel."

"I couldn't agree more."

"I'd like to wring that little worm's neck in my bare hands." She was mixing the cement but good now.

"Yes, I know. I feel exactly the same way. But I think it's probably in our best interest to pay him off. It might save you and your father a lot of money in the long run."

"If he ever steps foot in this place again, I'll break every bone in his body. I'll splatter his guts all over the city."

"I don't think he intends to." I wondered if she heard what I was saying. I felt like I was interrupting a fantasy disembowelment of Bill Walters every time I spoke.

"Here's the problem," I said, trying to get her back on track. "I'm supposed to meet him in an hour. He wants"—I coughed— "twenty-five thousand dollars. Half from you and half from Arnold Long."

"Where is he?" she asked. Just like that. No outrage. "Is he there with you now?"

"No. He called me from his apartment. We're supposed to meet him at the Paradise Room."

"That place is awful," she said.

I thought it was a peculiar moment for a restaurant review, but I hadn't noticed anything about Faith Wyder yet that wasn't peculiar.

"So you see why I was calling your father," I said. "Do you want to ask him if he's willing to pay?"

"No, not now. He's in a session."

I was getting impatient. If I hadn't been so incredulous, I would have been very impatient. "When will the session be over?"

"Not for a while. They usually last pretty long. You know." She paused. Just long enough for me to lose my temper and just short enough for me not to have time to say anything about it. "But we'll pay the money. I can make that decision. I'm the vice-president of the company. As long as you think it's the right thing to do."

Well, hallelujah. I was almost too dumbfounded to speak.

"I don't think we really have any choice," I managed.

"OK. As long as you promise to tell that fucking worm he doesn't have a job here anymore."

"I don't think he's planning on coming into work tomorrow."

"Do you want me to messenger it to you?"

"No. We'll come by and pick it up. We're on our way." Yes, indeed. Right now. Before you have time to change your mind, and before your mind has time to change itself.

"I'll be waiting for you, Renzler. Will the big guy be coming over with you?"

You bet your ass he will, sweetheart. If you like, I might even be able to persuade him to smack you around a little.

On the way over, I told Nate that we may have judged Faith Wyder too harshly. But when it came time to actually go inside the Nook and pick up the cash, we flipped a coin.

I lost.

No problem. Faith was "indisposed," Minnie Mouse said. But she had left the money right there on the reception desk, all wrapped up in a tight little bundle like a hunk of Swiss cheese. I opened it up and counted it, just to make sure a little rat hadn't eaten any.

She hadn't. That figured. Minnie looked like the sort of girl who doesn't buy anything without a credit card. In case it seems like I'm being a little hard on the poor girl, by the way, let me add this: She had a rock the size of Gibraltar on her hand and fingernails longer than french fries. She was painting them when I came in—black.

Things didn't go quite so easy over at Eden. Arnold Long was waiting for us in the Sanctuary, with Arnie right by his side. I had a feeling he had talked to Dad about my phone manner. This time there was no show of hospitality. No offer of a sauna or a massage. No invitation to the party.

I don't think we even would have gotten a drink, if I hadn't forced the issue.

"First of all," Arnold Long began, "I have to know what this money is for."

"Of course," I said. I didn't wait to see if he wanted to get to second-of-all and third-of-all right away. "It's for little Benedict Arnold, your ex-PR man, Bill Walters."

"Walters!" The name exploded from Arnold's mouth in a cloud of cigar smoke. "What does that moron have to do with this?"

I laid out the scenario as fast as I could, pausing here and there to allow Long the privilege of inserting expletives. I had to pause a lot. I told him we were supposed to meet his ex-PR man in half an hour. I didn't bother to tell him where. No need to rub it in.

Arnold's son remained strangely silent throughout my report. But when I was done, it was Arnie who let fire with a round of opposition.

"That's ridiculous," he shouted. "We're not going to pay him one red cent." He turned to face Arnold. "Are we, Dad?"

"I sure the hell don't want to." Long's voice was quiet, but I could tell he was seething with anger. "Did that scumball Wyder go along with all this?"

I nodded. I didn't see any reason to explain that Long's nemesis had been in a session when I called. For one thing, I had a feeling Arnold hadn't been getting any lately. At least, that's what Marla and Mindi seemed to think. But mostly I wanted to get the goddamn money and get the hell out of there as fast as we could.

"If we pay all this money to Walters, then what are we paying you for? Isn't that right, Dad?"

Arnold seemed to ignore his son's remark, so I did, too.

"So you think it's a good idea to give it to him," Long said to me.

"No, I think it's a lousy idea. But I think we really don't have much choice. You could call the cops on him. But then you get the police involved—"

"No, no. I don't want that."

"We could rough him up a little, if that makes you feel any better," Nate said.

Long shook his head.

"Dad doesn't believe in violence," Arnie explained.

"Dial him on the phone for me, Arnie. If he's going to get my money, he's going to get my two cents, too."

Arnie walked obediently across the room and circumnavigated his father's fig leaf desk. He must have had Walters' phone number memorized, because he started pressing buttons without hesitation. He picked up the box and carried it to his father. It was brand spanking new. I wondered how long this one would last.

"Walters," Arnold barked into the phone without introducing himself. I was sure Walters knew who it was. He was probably shaking like a plate of Jell-O. "I'm paying you your stinking money, Judas. But let me tell you that you are the lowest scum I have ever met in my entire life. And believe me, you little rat, I have met some scum in my time."

I stared out into space to avoid Nate's smirk. I think it was the Judas reference that got to him. If Walters was Judas, that made Arnold Jesus Christ.

Fine by me. It looked like we were about to get the money and go. Now, if we could just get out of there without a sermon.

Arnold slammed down the receiver without breaking the phone and reached into the pocket of his bathrobe. I thought he was grabbing for another cigar. I was wrong. He pulled out a wad of bills. My annual income. For some reason, I didn't feel too bad for the guy.

Arnie stood up. "Well, I just want it to go on record that I was entirely opposed to this idea." I wondered if the room was bugged and someone was taking minutes. He looked at his watch. "And now, if you two gentlemen don't mind, I have an appointment to go to."

We didn't answer, which I think he took to mean we couldn't have cared less. He was right.

"Don't mind Arnie," Long said to us after watching his son leave. "He's young, he's brash. And I think it's been very difficult for him, growing up being the son of a father who's an international celebrity. He wants to make the same kind of contribution to society that I have, but let's face it: Very few men get the opportunity to accomplish what I've done. And even if they do get the opportunity, very few of them have what it takes to make the most of it."

He began to peel some bills off the wad in his hand. "I'd pay anything to get Sherri back," he said quietly.

I nodded and took the money from him. "Maybe this will be the ticket."

"I hope so. That girl gives the best blow job a man ever had."

CHAPTER 21

We stopped to give our apologies to the girls and begged them to remain on standby until we returned from the Paradise Room. They offered to drive us over to Clark Street, but we declined. The Mercedes was illegally parked outside.

Lincoln Park West was lined with unmarked police cars and plain clothes cops when we got into our car. On the way over to Eden, we had seen a group of maybe 250 hippies gathering in the park for the evening's festivities. Unless more of them started arriving fast, the Days of Rage march was going to be a smaller affair than your average Italian wedding.

Chicago cops were stationed throughout the streets around the perimeter of the sprawling park. They outnumbered the protestors by probably ten to one. It looked like Mayor Daley could get out the foot soldiers a lot better than this Rudd kid everyone was talking about. The word in the papers was that the cops were eager for combat, because some of the hippies had blown up the police monument in Haymarket Square on Monday. After what had happened at the convention the year before, I had a feeling the cops didn't need any special incentive to bust hippies' heads. And I didn't need a weatherman to tell me that the protestors were going to get their asses kicked if they got out of line.

Over at the Paradise Room, there was no sign that a revolutionary war was about to start a few blocks away in the park. There also was no sign of Bill Walters.

It was 7:15. We were running a few minutes late. But I didn't think Walters would get impatient and leave. I also figured he'd be on time.

We ambled over to the bar, where Helene, the Cherub I'd passed the time with on my first mission to the joint, was chatting it up with a group of conventioneers. She jiggled her way to our end of the bar, leaving the boys from Iowa in a lurch. She remembered me from our first meeting, which meant she had a good memory.

Out of curiosity, I asked if Cindi West was working.

"No, she ain't here. She called in sick today." She laughed. "Probably just a hangover, knowing Cindi."

We laughed along with her. One round finished, and still no sign of Walters. There was no answer when I called his house. I was starting to get that feeling I get when my stomach starts to tell me something's wrong. We flagged Helene for a refill.

"Oh, I almost forgot," she said. "Your name ain't Pablo, is it?" I looked at Nate. Nate looked at me. "Cindi said if Pablo came in, tell him to go to her place."

Suddenly, I knew what the feeling in my stomach was all about.

"Thanks," I said. "Where does Cindi live again?"

"Lincoln Avenue."

"No, I know that. I just can't remember the number."

"Nineteen fifteen."

"That's right, nineteen fifteen."

We got out of there fast, but we left a pair of Alexander Hamiltons on the bar to keep Helene company.

"Where to now?" Nate asked when we got outside. That was the question of the minute.

"Pablo hasn't stopped in looking for Cindi, so maybe he's still out on the prowl," I answered. "I think we swing by Walters' place first."

"Yeah," Nate said. "There's always the possibility that Pablo's out prowling for Walters."

I nodded. "That thought did cross my mind."

Nate checked the map. "Cindi's place is closer, but Walters' place is close, too."

But not close enough.

When we got to Astor Street, where Bill Walters lived, there was a crowd of people in front of his building. I could see half a dozen cops in the crowd. Their cars were blocking the street.

An ambulance was parked beyond the cop cars. Bill Walters was parked next to the ambulance.

Two paramedics were putting a sheet over him when we reached the edge of the crowd. I managed to get the attention of an elderly rubbernecker who was watching the proceedings intently.

"What happened?" I asked.

"He jumped out his window." The man pointed up at the high rise. "Just like that." He snapped his fingers. "My wife saw the whole thing." He pointed at a woman standing ten feet away. "Hillary, come over here," he shouted. "Didn't you see the whole thing?"

Yessir, Hillary saw the whole thing. "He jumped," she said, as if to verify her eyewitness status. "Just like that."

"Did you actually *see* him standing up there before he jumped?"

Hillary wasn't entirely sure. "Yes, but he wasn't standing up there. He just came outside and jumped. Just like that."

Just like that.

We walked back toward the car. "Pushed," Nate said. "Or maybe stuffed full of acid and then he jumped."

"Or maybe pushed, or maybe both," I said. "By tomorrow morning, we'll probably be able to get a police report."

Nate started the car. "Where to now, private eye? On to Cindi West's apartment?"

"I was thinking," I said.

"Good for you. It's excellent exercise. Like push-ups for the brain."

"Did it seem to you that Arnie Long was in a hurry to leave Eden?"

Nate lit a cigarette. We were still parked at the curb, engine running. "I was so relieved when he left, I didn't really notice. But now that you mention it . . ."

"Walters didn't jump without someone's help," I said. "If it was Pablo who helped, I wonder who tipped him off."

"Perhaps young Arnie Long?"

I nodded. "I wonder where Arnie is now. I wonder if there's anything interesting in his office."

"There's one way to find out."

We flipped a coin again. This time, I won. Or at least it seemed that way at the time.

I elected to visit Cindi West while Nate went off to search Arnie Long's office. I was sacrificing an opportunity to see Marla, but with any luck there'd be plenty of time for that later. If things went well tonight, we'd be able to get into bed and not get out of it until the World Series started on Saturday. Besides, we did only have a physical relationship.

Close or not, it turned out to be a long ride to Cindi West's apartment. The cops were rerouting traffic at North Avenue, which runs along the south side of Lincoln Park. Figure that one out, city planning buffs. From our vantage, we could see a throng of hippies huddled around a bonfire to keep warm. Some of them were wearing football helmets. Smart move. If I were planning on marching, I would have ordered a suit of chain mail. We had to double back behind a line of crawling cars to Division Street and then cut north again on Wells. By the time Nate dropped me off on Lincoln Avenue, it was pushing 9 P.M.

Cindi lived in an OK neighborhood, but her three-story walkup wasn't exactly a security building. There was no doorman to contend with, and the lobby door didn't close tightly. I made it up the two flights to her apartment unannounced, without having to pull any sleight-of-tongue or hand.

I stood outside the door to her apartment, listening for possible evidence that Cindi might have company. I could hear a radio playing a Beatles song and a female voice humming along. She was about half an octave from the right key. I waited for the song to end. The only voice I could hear belonged to a hyped-up disc jockey.

Cindi wasn't expecting me, so I didn't expect her to open the door when I knocked. She didn't.

"Who is it?" A reasonable question. I hoped she might ask, "Is that you, Pablo?" and give herself away. But Helene had pretty much taken care of giving her away already.

"It's Mark Renzler." I didn't see any advantage in using deception. But a little cajoling wouldn't hurt. "You remember me, the private detective who was looking for your sister? The innocent guy?"

She remembered all right. And judging by the tone of her voice, it wasn't a fond memory. "What do you want? How'd you get in?"

I answered the second question first. "I walked up the stairs. The lock on the door's broken. I want to ask you a couple of questions."

"I don't feel like answering any questions."

"Please. It's about your sister."

No answer.

Time for a little deception. "I got a report that someone saw her in St. Louis. I just want to speak with you a minute before I go off on a wild goose chase." I'll bet that one confused her.

She started to speak, then hesitated, then said, "I don't have any clothes on."

I was starting to make a little progress. "I don't mind," I said. But I thought maybe she did, so I added, "Waiting for you to change, I mean."

"Hah! Funny guy." But not funny enough to be let in.

I tried the pleading approach. "It would save me a lot of time. I'd really appreciate it if you'd just open the door and talk to me. It will only take a minute. I won't come in. I promise."

That was a lie. I wanted to be inside that apartment and looking at her face to face when I mentioned the name Pablo Johnson. I wanted her to be looking at me when I told her how many years someone can get for being an accomplice to kidnapping and extortion. The next step was to start picking the lock.

It wasn't necessary. I had expected her to keep the chain lock on if she did open the door. I had one foot braced against it and the other one ready to kick it in. That wasn't necessary, either.

For some reason, she relented. It turned out to be a good

reason, from her point of view. It didn't have anything to do with my silver tongue or my dashing looks.

The door swung open and I could see that Cindi had been lying about not being dressed. But it was only a little white lie. All she had on was a short see-through negligee that seemed a little skimpy for a chilly October night when the landlords are still holding back on providing their tenants with heat. I stepped inside and occupied myself with seeing through to her goose bumps. At the same moment, the reason she had decided to let me in became suddenly clear, like a thought that dawns on you in the far back of your head.

That's exactly where it dawned on me.

Either my hearing was going bad or Pablo Johnson and Cindi West didn't have a whole lot to talk about. I didn't get a look at him, of course, but I figured he was the one who had been stationed behind the door and was now using my head for target practice.

At first glancing blow, he seemed like a pretty good shot. But after the second shot, I had reason to believe he was taking aim from very short range. I wasn't awake to feel the third blow, if there was a third.

I never did figure out what the hell the bastard hit me with.

CHAPTER 22

$\mathbf{S}$ometimes after getting clob- bered over the head, you notice the small things first.

Like your shoelaces. One of mine was untied. It must have come lose during my smashing entrance number.

And the time. There was a tiny pink clock on the night table in Cindi's bedroom. It was a tiny bedroom. The night table was pink. The whole damn bedroom was pink. According to the clock—and when have you ever seen a pink clock that didn't work?—it was 9:20. That meant I had been out for maybe ten minutes. That's about what it felt like.

I checked my watch for a second opinion. It was then that I noticed my hands were bound with electrical tape. That stuff's a pain in the ass to get off, believe me. Especially when your hands are tied behind your back.

I was sitting more or less upright on the floor, slumped back against a wall that felt cold through my leather jacket. I'd say it took me probably two minutes to notice that there was another tenant in the bedroom. This was especially slow reaction time, considering she wasn't wearing anything except a pair of panties. She must have really been feeling the chill.

Like me, she was tied into a short-term lease. Only she was under a gag order. I wasn't. I wondered why.

It didn't take me long to find out.

Within a minute or so, Pablo Johnson came into the bedroom

behind Cindi West. It was the first time I had met him in the flesh. He wasn't a pretty sight. For sheer greasiness, none of the photos I had seen did justice to his clean-cut appearance. He was either in bad need of a shave or a complete failure at trying to grow a beard. His eyes were glazed like a sugar donut. Someone—Moses Godley, I think it was—told me Pablo had taken too many acid trips. That was a diagnosis I was willing to believe.

Pablo was holding a gun in his hand. *My* gun. The gun I should have been carrying in *my* hand when I entered Cindi's apartment. One of these days I'm finally going to learn to stop underestimating women. Especially women who hang around with guys like Pablo.

He spoke to my roommate first. "What do you think of that, Sherri?" he said. "We brought you some company so you wouldn't get lonely. Did he introduce himself or should I do it?"

"We've met before," I told him. I smiled at Sherri. "It's kind of like a reunion, but I'm not sure she remembers."

Sherri began to nod forcefully. I stand corrected. She did remember me.

I was waking up a bit now, but I still wasn't functioning at peak efficiency. I scoped the place out slowly in an effort to get my bearings. I was sitting in the farthest corner of the room from the doorway, along the wall near the foot of the bed. Sherri was sitting to my left in the other corner along the same wall. She was about six feet from the door. There was another door in the room, the fire escape. It was probably eight feet away along the wall to my right, the wall opposite the doorway. That was the one through which I'd be making my exit if I got the chance.

At the moment, it didn't look like I'd be getting the chance.

Sherri's older sister took five steps toward me, which pretty much brought her all the way across the room. Since the last time I had seen her, she had slipped into something more uncomfortable—a pair of jeans that was two sizes too small and one of those scratchy denim workshirts. She kneeled down beside me and put one of her hands behind my neck. She began stroking the back of my head.

"Jesus, you hit him hard, Pablo," she said. "You could have killed the guy." She kissed my head. "Poor baby."

I was about to thank her for her concern when she tried to stuff the pills into my mouth.

Peak efficiency or not, I sure the hell wasn't falling for that trick. I made sure she felt sorry for trying it. I bit into the fleshy underside of her thumb and held on like I was breaking into a bag of potato chips without following the E-Z open instructions.

She let out a yelp and dropped the pills, scattering them onto the floor and under the bed. They were tiny purple pills. I had never seen LSD before, but I didn't need to check the *Physician's Desk Reference* to figure out that was what they were.

Cindi fell back onto the bed clutching her hand. She yelped for a few seconds, then stood up in a rage. "You bastard," she screamed. She took a step forward and swung at me with an open right hand. It landed, even though I ducked a bit. Nothing to call the paramedics about, but her nails did a pretty good number on my ear. Not as good a job as I had done on her hand, however.

Pablo was leaning against the wall all the while, taking in the scene with a bemused expression on his goofy face. Now he moved slowly forward, stepping over Cindi, who was down on all fours picking up the pills.

"OK, pig." He spoke in the voice of a kid who started practicing Jimmy Cagney imitations at the age of twelve and never got any better. "We tried it Cindi's way. Now we do it my way. Cindi's gonna give you the acid again. Only this time, if you don't take it down, I'm gonna shoot you." He waved the gun for effect, but it was clear he wasn't accustomed to handling firearms.

"You're not going to shoot me, asshole," I answered. "You've got to do this quietly. Otherwise, you're going to have a body in Cindi's apartment to get rid of but fast. And you're going to have to find another place to keep Sherri for the evening. That would be awfully inconvenient."

Friends have accused me of being sarcastic to the point of disbelief in the narration of my close calls. And they're right. I do have a tendency to exaggerate my coolness under pressure. So to set the record straight: I was scared stiff sitting in that room. I had seen Steve Farrell and I had seen Whitey Howard. I didn't have any desire to join them in the vegetable garden. I had no way of knowing for sure that Pablo Johnson wasn't insane enough to pull the trigger. But still, that's exactly what I said to him.

Pablo's expression didn't vary much, but Cindi looked as nervous as a rookie facing Sandy Koufax in his first big-league at-bat.

"He's right, Pablo," she said. "We can't shoot him."

"Stay cool. Let me do the thinking."

"Maybe he doesn't care," I said to Cindi. "After all, it's not *his* apartment."

"Shut up," he said to me.

"Put the gun down, Pablo."

"Shut up," he repeated. This time he was talking to Cindi.

He tried to stare me down. When that didn't work, he pointed the gun at my head. His hand was shaking.

"You better use two hands if you plan on hitting me."

That got him mad. And got me a kick in the ribs. Lucky for me all the hippies were wearing sneakers these days.

"You motherfucker," he shouted. "You think I don't have the guts to do it."

I shrugged. "Even if you did, it wouldn't matter." Time to play my ace. Time to really rattle the jerk. "The gun doesn't work without bullets in it. The gun doesn't have any bullets in it. Therefore, the gun doesn't work."

I didn't think it was necessary to add that the bullets were hidden in the top part of my sock. This was a precaution I started taking a few years back following another occasion when I was dumb enough to let someone take away my gun. A dame was involved that time, too.

"Goddamnit!" Pablo was finally getting some color in his face. His whole body was shaking with rage, and the hand without the gun in it was clenched into a tight fist. The spasm stopped after about fifteen seconds, and he began to glare at me.

"Bullshit!" he said finally. A smile was beginning to spread over his face.

"Go ahead, sharpshooter, pull the trigger." I smiled. "You'll see."

"Put down the gun," Cindi said. Her voice was quivering. "Let's just try to get the acid into him."

"Shut up." Pablo was trying to check the gun.

"If you untie my hands, I'll be glad to show you how to open it," I said.

Well, that did it.

Pablo threw the gun down on the bed and shouted, "Fuckin' A." At least I think that's what he said. I had never heard the expression before. I think it might be exclusive to the Midwest.

"Give me the fuckin' acid," he demanded, holding out his hand to Cindi. She complied with his order, and he came rushing toward me.

It wasn't much fun getting banged against the wall, but it was exactly what I'd been hoping for. If Pablo had any sense, he would have simply knocked me out cold and then dosed me. I had succeeded in goading him on so bad that he elected to go the hard route.

The odds were still in his favor, of course, but they weren't overwhelming. He was probably twenty-five pounds lighter than I am, and he was built like the kid who's always the last one picked when you're choosing up sides for a game.

He hurled himself on top of me, cramming me into the corner. He was grabbing at my head with his right hand and trying to stuff the pills into my mouth with his left. I resisted by pressing my weight back against him and keeping my mouth shut as tight as a Mafia kingpin testifying before the grand jury. So far it was working.

"Come on, get over here, help me," he yelled at Cindi.

"What do you want me to do?" Her voice was hysterical.

"Hold down his legs," he instructed.

Cindi found out the hard way that it wasn't as easy as it sounded. But Pablo had succeeded in pushing me down to the floor. Gravity was working in their favor now. It took a few moments, but Pablo finally got into a kneeling position on my chest.

"Here, you take the acid," he said to Cindi. "I'll try to pry his mouth open."

That wasn't as easy as it sounded, either. But I knew I couldn't hold out much longer. He was covering my nose with his top hand. Sooner or later, I had to breathe.

I felt three pills go in, but I managed to spit two of them back out. In the process, one went down. Better to swallow one, I figured, than to start choking and open the way for more. She forced two more in, but I was able to reject one of them.

Nate said they had given Steve Farrell six. I figured I had probably reached my limit. I summoned all my strength and pushed up, driving Pablo backward. He lost his balance and tumbled off my chest, granting me a momentary reprieve. It turned out to be longer than momentary.

When he whirled to regain his balance, he noticed that Sherri had checked out of the room without leaving a forwarding address. I could have told him that thirty seconds before, if he had only given me a chance to speak.

"Sherri! Get Sherri!" he sputtered, pointing frantically at the doorway.

On second thought, he decided to go himself. I tried to trip him as he pulled away, but he was a bit more agile than I expected. He stumbled out of the room after Cindi, who had been a little slow getting out of the starting gate herself. I could hear him issuing new orders when he caught up with her in the next room.

"I'll get Sherri. You stand by the door," he commanded. "If he tries to get out, hit him with this."

"This" turned out to be a ceramic vase that Cindi had probably made herself during high school. If it was any later than high school, she needed to get herself checked out for retardation as soon as possible.

Getting out of there was, as Nate would say, "a piece of cake." An exaggeration perhaps, but I was, after all, fighting for my life.

She was waiting by the doorway. I surprised her by going right for the fire escape. By the time she got around the bed and across the room, I had the deadbolt turned. She swung wildly with the vase, and I ducked away. That was the only swing she got. I kicked her once in the leg and caught her in the stomach with my knee as she fell down. To make sure she didn't get up, I kicked her one more time—in the spot where I've never touched another woman with anything but the utmost tender loving care.

Turning the door knob took some maneuvering, but I've got the hands of a second baseman. As I stepped out onto the fire escape, I could hear Pablo returning to the apartment. I figured he must have caught up with Sherri, because he hadn't been gone long enough to have given up the search. Plus she hadn't gotten a very big head start.

For a moment, I thought about waiting outside the door and taking Pablo out with a sneak attack. But I thought the drugs might hamper me, and then I thought maybe it was the drugs that were making me think I should go back inside and be a hero. I was starting to get a buzzing sensation in my head. Was that the drugs or was it the pounding I had taken?

I moved cautiously down the first flight of stairs, the only flight of stairs. I had a decision to make when I got to the second-floor landing. It wasn't that long a jump down to the alley—not when your hands aren't tied behind your back, that is. It would be a whole lot shorter jump if I could get them in front of me. Of course, that's not such an easy proposition, either. Unless you've got some time to kill.

I didn't. Pablo bounded out the fire escape door and looked down at me. He paused for a moment, then started down the stairs.

I decided on option three. A few yards ahead of me in the alley below was a dumpster. Not your standard size trash bin, but one of those enormous containers that you see all over Manhattan taking up valuable parking spaces. I've never been able to figure out what they're used for—maybe for Con Edison repair guys to keep their lunch pails in.

At any rate, I finally found a worthwhile use for one. In the dark, I couldn't tell what was in it. Only that it was full.

Dirt. It turned out to be filled with dirt. I've never been a big dirt fan, but it felt like a Hollywood bath when I landed in it. I'd been expecting maybe old boards with rusty nails in them. I didn't take the time to dust myself off, because Pablo was on the landing. He was trying to muster up the balls to jump.

Once again, I thought about waiting him out. Once again, I wondered if it was the drugs talking to me. Once again, I felt the buzzing sensation in my head.

When I hit the street, I suddenly felt like I had a lot of extra spring in my step. I used it to carry me down the alley as fast as I could go.

CHAPTER 23

You could travel the entire city of Chicago just sticking to the alleys. It's almost like a whole other world back there. It's a maze of dirty brick walls and drab gray stairways, darker and narrower and colder and quieter. It would make a fascinating tour sometime. But not tonight, thank you.

I cut left down the first alley I hit. The only sound I could hear was the pounding of my feet on the cobblestone and the echo of the pounding of my feet, and just maybe the pounding of Pablo Johnson's feet far behind me. I had a good lead to start with and I felt like I was extending it with each stride I took.

Two packs of butts a day will catch up with you. But the night seemed so tranquil and the chilly air seemed so refreshing that I was beginning to feel like I could keep running and never stop. It was right about then that the dog started barking.

He sounded like a big dog. Pardon my sexism, ladies, but I always think of big dogs as hes. He was stationed behind a fence to my right. I instinctively moved to my left and stumbled into a row of garbage cans.

So much for tranquility. So much for darkness. It might have been my imagination, but it seemed like everyone on the block turned on the porch lights to see what was going on. In New York, they would have pulled down the shades.

The sense of rhythm I had built up vanished as I regained my balance and lumbered away. I heard a car turn into the alley back at the corner and could feel its headlights warming my back. I wondered if Pablo had decided on a different line of pursuit. I turned right down the next alley I hit. I could see street lights flickering about ninety feet ahead of me. That's the distance between third and the plate. And all the other bases, for that matter.

I heard the car coming up the other alley. It slowed down for a moment. Just long enough to make me turn on the jets. Then it kept on going.

Home free.

It was a wide, bright street. I stopped and took a long look back into the darkness behind me. No sign of Pablo Johnson. I turned right and started to walk. Two blocks ahead of me, I could see the edge of the park.

A middle-aged couple was walking toward me. I thought about asking them what street I was on, but they crossed over to the other side. I had a feeling they wanted to get away from me.

At the first cross street, I found out where I was.

Armitage. That meant the Nook was nearby. That's about all it meant. I had gotten to know Chicago a little bit in the three or four times I'd been there, but tonight I was all turned around. I wonder why.

It didn't matter. All I had to do was flag down a cab and ask to be dropped at the Drake. But it's tough to hail a cab with your arms tied behind your back. Three hippie types passed by and stared at me like I had just escaped from prison. If only they knew.

I ducked into the next alley and hid behind a dumpster. I moved my arms to the front. That's not as easy as it sounds. Try it some time when you've got a few minutes.

My new look wouldn't stop people from staring, but at least I'd be able to flag down a cab. But it's tough to hail cabs when there aren't any. It's even tougher when you don't have any money.

Shit. I checked my pockets as well as I could. I still had my cigarettes, but no matches. And not one stinking cent.

I was coming up close to the park now. I still had the spring in my step, and my hands were starting to tingle. Was that the drugs speeding up my circulation or the tape cutting it off? I suppose I could have put the question to a cop. There were plenty of them there to ask.

They were lined up on the far side of the wide street next to the park. Clark Street, I found out it was when I reached the corner. Some of the cops were in plain clothes, most of them were in uniform. Quite a few of them were wearing helmets. Some were sitting in their cars, most were standing next to them. The ones who were standing were chatting with each other or jabbering into walkie-talkies. If you were looking for a cop, this was as good a time and place as you could ever pick.

I thought about crossing the street and asking one of them for a dime to make a phone call. I decided that would be a bad idea. None of them looked very busy, but you could tell they were waiting for a war to start. I didn't want to be the first casualty.

I turned right on Clark and kept walking. There was no way I was going to cross over into that park.

I planned on asking the first person I saw who didn't look like a cop for a dime. But the street was deserted except for people who looked like cops. I had a feeling a lot of people had decided to avoid the park that night. Smart thinking.

All of a sudden, I saw a dime on the sidewalk about ten feet ahead of me. I speeded up, thinking I should get to it before someone else did. It was sparkling in the reflection of the street light. All of a sudden, the whole sidewalk was glittering with dimes. I could make a hundred phone calls if I wanted to.

When I reached down to pick one up, it wasn't there. I think I found out what a hallucination is.

Across the street to my left I could see the bonfire blazing in the park. It looked like it was miles away, and then it seemed like I could almost reach out and touch it. But I knew that was a hallucination, so I didn't try. And then I thought, if it wasn't a hallucination, I'd burn my hand.

Beyond the bonfire I could see the lights of cars on a highway. That would be Lake Shore Drive. I pretty much knew where I was now, but it was a long walk to the Drake Hotel.

There were more protestors gathered around the bonfire now, a lot more. It looked like there were thousands of them. They were chanting and shouting slogans, and a guy was giving a speech through a bullhorn. I could hear war whoops, like the Indian soundtracks in an Audie Murphy movie. I wanted to stop and watch and listen. But I kept feeling that buzzing sensation in my head, and it was telling me to keep moving, to get out of there fast.

Up ahead, I could see a telephone booth. I didn't think it was a hallucination. To make sure, I walked up to it and touched it with my hand. But what good is a pay phone without a dime? I turned and looked at the building behind me.

Moody Bible Institute. I thought about going inside and asking for a show of Christian charity. But I had my pride. I didn't want to feel like a wino in Grand Central Station.

I felt sheepish doing it, but I went inside the phone booth and pushed the coin return lever. Just like a wino in Grand Central.

The lever felt soft in my fingers. I heard a coin drop into the return tray. Or did I?

I did. Indeed I did. Praise the Lord.

I picked out the dime and held it gingerly between my thumb and forefinger. I had to look at it to make sure it was there. The noise from the park sounded like it was getting closer. I could hear everything very clearly.

A bus rattled down Clark Street and I felt the phone booth shake. I shuddered. It was cold all of a sudden. I looked at the bonfire in the distance and began to warm up. Hurry up and make that goddamn call.

It wasn't until I pulled the receiver off the hook that I noticed the hand-lettered sign on the Big Mac wrapper taped over the coin slot: Out of order.

At least in Chicago somebody makes the effort to put up a sign, I thought. Probably the guy who lost his dime.

A couple of blocks ahead, I could see a restaurant. There'd be a phone there. All I had to do was get across one big intersection without losing my dime. It was melting into my fingers.

I wanted to turn and watch the bonfire, stop and listen to the Indians. I put my head down and kept walking. When I reached the intersection, the light was red, bright red. There were no cars coming, but I thought I should wait until the light turned green. I was afraid a cop would see me and give me a ticket for jaywalking.

It seemed like I was waiting there a long time. All around me I could hear the voices of cops coming over those goddamn radios. Where were all the cars? Where were all the people?

A woman and a man crossed the intersection. They weren't worried about getting a ticket. I started to step off the curb, but a car came by. All of a sudden, out of nowhere.

When the light changed, I ran across the street. I kept on running until I got to the restaurant.

As soon as I stepped inside, I began to feel like I couldn't breathe. The warmth of the place was cutting off my air supply. It felt so crowded in there, but there were only a few people. The lights were so bright, I had to cover my eyes. I caught sight of a case filled with pies and felt nauseated. I wanted to go back outside and get a drink of cold air.

A guy standing behind the cashier's desk was staring at me. I thought maybe I should explain why my hands were tied. I started to, then stopped. I didn't think he was interested, anyway.

I asked him where the phone was, and he pointed to the doorway I had just come through. I turned around in disbelief, but goddamn if he wasn't right. I crushed the receiver in my hand when I took it off the hook. It seemed like it took a full minute to dial O. Suddenly, I wanted a cigarette. I fished one out of my pocket while waiting for the operator. I could see a pack of matches in the bottom of the cigarette machine. It was right next to the phone. Where was that goddamn operator?

I grabbed for the matches while holding the phone against my chest with my elbow. It was awkward lighting the cigarette with my hands tied. They were tingling so much. It seemed like it took a long time. But I had to have one right away.

Her voice sounded like she was yelling at me. Maybe she was. How long did I make her wait?

I asked for the Drake Hotel. She told me I could dial it direct.

I told her I was blind.

Pretty good line, I thought. I was grinning so wide my jaw ached. I took a drag off my cigarette. Ah, fresh air.

When the voice on the phone said, "Drake Hotel," I felt like he was welcoming me back from the dead. I remembered waking up in the hospital after the operation on my eye and seeing my mother and father and my teammate, Randy McGee, smiling at me. I was going to be OK. I wondered what happened to Randy. I hadn't talked to Randy in six years. How did it get to be so long ago? Last I heard he was living back in South Carolina.

Then Nate got on the line. I thought he had the nicest voice I'd heard since the days when my mother used to call me in for dinner after I'd been out playing ball all day. I started to tell him that, but he asked me what was wrong.

I guess I wasn't making as much sense as I thought I was.

I told him I was in trouble. Pablo slipped me some acid, but I didn't really feel that bad. I felt pretty good, in fact, now that I was talking to him.

"How much did he give you?" Nate's voice was scared. That wasn't right. Nate never sounds scared.

"Two pills," I said. "Two purple ones. Don't worry. They were real small."

He breathed a sigh of relief. I could hear it. He sounded like he was right next to me. I began trying to light another cigarette. Damn, that last one tasted good.

"Microdot," he said.

I didn't know what he was talking about.

"I think you're going to be OK," he said. "Are you sure you only took two?"

"Positive. Two. I feel fine," I said. "Just great, as a matter of fact."

"Where are you?"

Uh, good question.

"Let's see. I was on Clark Street . . . Yeah, I think I'm on Clark Street."

Another voice came on the line. The operator. Suddenly, I didn't feel so good anymore.

"Your three minutes are up," she said. "You'll have to deposit—"

"But I don't have any more money." Even in my altered state, I realized that was the dumbest fucking thing I could possibly have said. I started pleading with her. *"Please."*

"No, goddamnit. This is an emergency." Nate's voice again. "Reverse the charges. Do whatever the hell you have to. Just don't cut him off."

He was yelling. Nate almost never yells.

"Where are you?" He was yelling at me now.

Something told me I better figure out where the hell I was or I was going to be in deep, deep shit.

I looked at the guy behind the cashier's desk. His face was distorted, like it was made of putty. "Where am I?"

He gave me a look like I was nuts and held up a menu. I had to strain to make out the letters.

I had never failed an eye examination before, even after I lost the sight in one of them. But then the letters on the eye chart aren't moving when they give you the exam. I was straining so hard I could feel the muscles working in my temples. I got the letters to stop moving, but they still didn't make any sense. It was like doing the jumble puzzle in the newspaper, next to the horoscopes.

For one fleeting moment, I was able to unscramble them. "Mitchell's," I shouted. "The Original Mitchell's."

"Stay right there," Nate commanded. "Don't move." Then, in the softest, sweetest, most soothing voice I've ever heard, he said, "Don't worry, Renz, we'll find the place."

CHAPTER 24

My name is Nate Moore, and I agreed, albeit reluctantly, to assume the responsibility for the narration of this story until such time as my friend Mark Renzler had recovered sufficiently from his ingestion of LSD that he was capable of stringing together three or four sentences with at least some semblance of coherence.

I am hardly the stylistic wit that Renzler tends to be, although I can assure you that in getting the story from me, you will at least be assured of accuracy. Renzler has a marked tendency to sacrifice facts for flights of fancy, and while he manages to maintain a course that bears some approximation to the flow of the truth, you must read carefully between the lines to discern whether he is providing pertinent information or taking narrative liberties for the sake of entertainment.

You've probably also noticed an inclination toward long-windedness on occasion. You will get none of that from me.

When at last I found my friend on the evening of Wednesday, October 8, I was accompanied by Mindi and Marla, who are mentioned previously in the story. The latter, incidentally, had managed to cause a considerable stir in Renzler's loins, the likes of which I had not been witness to for at least two years. When I mentioned this observation to him, Renzler dismissed it as being "utterly ridiculous." But that does not invalidate it in any way; if anything, it substantiates it, because Renzler is quite possibly the most dismissive person I've ever encountered. He has a denial system that is second to none, save perhaps Richard Nixon's.

Locating Mitchell's, the restaurant from which Renzler had placed his desperately incoherent call, posed no difficulty at all, because Mindi had eaten there on numerous occasions before. It was getting there that presented a problem.

Renzler could not have picked a worse location to call from on that particular night; or a worse time, for that matter. Because at approximately 10:30, some 400 or so SDS, Weathermen and other militant protestors spilled out of Lincoln Park and began to charge through Chicago's Gold Coast, inflicting random damage on anything that got in their way. I subsequently found out that their intention had been to march down to the Drake Hotel, where Renzler and I were registered, to assert their rage at Julius Hoffman, the flinty conspiracy trial judge who provided so much entertainment for Renzler and myself when we had time to inhabit the hotel bar.

Ultimately, the demonstrators did not make it that far, thanks to some exceedingly forceful head-bashing at the hands of the Chicago police. But I am getting too far ahead of myself. Back to rescuing Renzler.

The restaurant he had chosen, or more appropriately, had stumbled into, was situated at the corner of North Avenue and Clark Street. Those of you who are familiar with Chicago will recognize this as being a mere stone's throw from the south end of Lincoln Park, the approximate site where the so-called National Action began. And I can assure you that many stones were thrown that night.

It took us more than half an hour to get there, averting the area of confrontation through Marla and Mindi's knowledge of Chicago geography and a bit of experimentation on the part of yours truly. We found our friend slumped in a booth, gulping down lemonade and staring out the window at the proceedings across the way.

When we entered, we were greeted by a putty-faced man who knew instantly that we were looking for Renzler. Perhaps Renzler had described me to him, although I can't imagine that Renzler was capable of it, considering his level of coherence in the phone conversation I had had with him. But he is a professional in these matters and capable of tremendous recall and reconstruction of detail.

"He had five Cokes and then he switched to lemonade," the putty-faced man told me. "He said you'd be willing to pay for them."

"Naturally," I assured him. My inclination was to punch the warthog in the nose, but I resisted. In fact, we wound up dining there, partially on account of Mindi's recommendation and mostly on account of my condition, which was hunger rapidly approaching starvation. But the proceedings outside were beginning to get a bit threatening, so we moved Renzler to a booth toward the back.

If you're ever in Chicago, exercise the liberty to pass on this establishment. I would recommend it highly to anyone I loathed. For one thing, there was no booze. For another, the menu had pictures of the entrees, which ranged from spaghetti to silver dollar pancakes.

As I said, I was extremely hungry, so I had a plate of spaghetti and two orders of silver dollar pancakes.

Having consumed two hits of acid, Renzler was not in any mood to partake of food. He was disinclined even to look at the pictures on the menu, which I'll readily admit did nothing to enhance my own appetite. He treated us to an account of his adventure with Pablo Johnson, which turned out to be quite amusing. The humor, I think, was largely due to his condition. I'll not recount the story for you here, because the version you've already read is undoubtedly more accurate, even if it is a bit lacking in amusement value.

You may wonder, I suppose, why I did not show much concern over Renzler's condition vis-à-vis the drugs. Let me assure you that I took great care to examine his bruises and scratches—as did the girls—immediately upon our arrival. I even went so far as to drag him off to the can to wash up. But I was pretty confident that two hits of LSD would do no long-term damage to any sane person. And in the case of Renzler, whom I have seen consume up to a quart of bourbon in one sitting—a long one, I'll grant you—I rather thought it might actually do some good. Two hits was more than I would have prescribed, of course, but once he recovered, I thought he might gain some valuable insight from the experience.

The timing, however, could not have been worse. What we both needed before our assignment the next day was a good night's rest. It was obvious that we were not going to get one. The girls, fortunately, were not without experience in the matter of all-nighters, and I was able to procure from them a sufficient quantity of amphetamines to provide me with the requisite energy to see Renzler through his first and, quite likely, only psychedelic experience. At forty-six years old, I am no longer able to stay up all night relying on Mother Nature's support alone.

By the time we were finished eating, Renzler was so far gone that a fork was providing all the stimulation he needed. As a result, he was largely oblivious to the skirmishes that were taking place out in the street between the weathermen and the police. Fortunately, we were on the periphery of the battle, the real war being fought farther south and to the east—in the direction of our hotel.

There was one incident in which it appeared as if a demonstrator would shatter the window of the restaurant—and the faces of a few curious patrons pressed against it—with a brick. But he was clubbed from behind by one of Chicago's finest before he could set his feet to throw. The proprietor took the precaution of locking the door while the would-be brick hurler and two of his comrades were being thrown into a paddy wagon. This surprised me a bit, because he seemed like the sort who would be standing at the ready with snack-sacks for the men in blue. (The restaurant appeared to be the sort that provided bottomless cups of complimentary coffee to them as a matter of policy.) And it struck me as being a bit foolish, since I've never seen a brick stop to open a door before coming through it.

When things had returned to a relative calm, I asked the man what the charge was for the insult and we made our way back to the car. Before returning to the hotel, however, I made one last-ditch effort to render our appointment in the zoo the next day null and void.

I was almost certain that Pablo Johnson had changed his headquarters as soon as Renzler escaped, but I've learned from Renzler that one cannot afford to make assumptions in his line of work. For the moment, it was my line of work as well. It did occur to me that I could have increased the odds on finding him if we had gone directly there before stopping to eat, but I also figured that if Johnson was stupid enough to stay at that apartment for one hour, he was quite possibly stupid enough to stay there for two or three.

In addition, I was famished. And in addition to that, Renzler is the professional, not me.

From Renzler's description of Cindi West's apartment, it sounded as if the fire escape would be the most auspicious location from which to mount a sneak attack. But also from his description of the place, it was impossible to ascertain which was the correct fire escape. Moreover, I was not planning a sneak attack. If Johnson was in that apartment, I didn't think I would have any trouble getting inside and tearing him limb from limb. I thought I'd rather enjoy it, actually.

I left the girls in the car to take care of Renzler and got the crowbar out of the trunk. Renzler would have picked the lock, but he's a finesse man and I'm not. He was fairly insistent about accompanying me into the building, and for a moment I almost considered letting him. But I managed to convince him that he would have a much better time if he stayed in the car and played with the fork that Marla had smuggled out of the restaurant in her purse.

Getting into the building and upstairs to the apartment was a piece of cake. The door to the domicile itself was not that formidable an obstacle, either. On another day, when I had no concern about the noise level, I could have gotten through it with my foot. I had heard a radio playing softly inside, so I raised the crowbar to my shoulder before I entered. It was highly unlikely, but I had to consider the possibility that Johnson was waiting inside with the same object he had used in his rear assault on Renzler.

He was not. Nor was Cindi West poised with her high school

ceramics project. It was clear that the pair had cleared out in a considerable hurry. Drawers had been left open and possessions were scattered about the floor. I checked the bedroom to make sure they had not forgotten Sherri in their haste to hit the road. I also conducted a perfunctory search for something of value.

I could find nothing that pertained to the case, as we detectives like to refer to it, but I did uncover a rather impressive stash of marijuana and a film cannister that was filled to the brim with microdot. Renzler is correct in saying that I am too old to indulge in drugs, although I tend to view it more as a matter of having been born too early. But I do have some younger friends who would be quite happy if I returned from Chicago with a collection of souvenirs. They say a few hits of acid makes a great stocking stuffer at Christmas.

I switched off the radio to conserve electricity and returned to the car. Renzler had lost interest in the fork, but the girls were singing songs to keep him entertained. Their rendition of "Satisfaction" left a lot to be desired, but it was unlikely that he was able to distinguish it from the original.

The girls were rather disappointed, as was Renzler, when I insisted on driving them home, but I thought it wise to save them and him any possible embarrassment that might arise in the event that his trip turned ugly. All Renzler needed to finish off his day was for a pair of twenty-two-year-olds to be on hand when he started babbling incoherently about his ex-wives.

That task completed, I drove west to the expressway, then south to Ohio Street to ensure that we did not venture into the war zone. Renzler contented himself with singing "Satisfaction." The guy was a great drunk, and so far he was turning out to be a great drug head. I wanted to get back into our hotel room before that changed.

We arrived just in time to put in a major beverage order with room service. When the waiter departed, I hung the DO NOT DISTURB sign on the door knob. These two boys had a big exam the next day, and they were settling in for an all-nighter.

CHAPTER 25

The good thing about drugs like speed and LSD is that they make the time fly by. The bad thing about them is that they make every second seem like a minute.

Those two statements might sound contradictory, but at the risk of sounding like a Zen master, I can tell you that they contain an essential kernel of truth that might explain in part the appeal of drugs to some, as well as the lack thereof to others. In addition, please bear in mind that the statements are being made by a man who was born in a shroud of ambivalence and lives in the cracks of paradox.

Hmm, that sounds rather good. I confess that I'm beginning to enjoy this writing stuff.

Renzler previously noted that our hotel window afforded an excellent view of Lake Shore Drive and the "Inner Drive," as Chicagoans are inclined to speak of it. I believe he likened it to a postcard, which is an accurate, if somewhat unimaginative, analogy. When we returned to our suite, the scene bore more resemblance to El Greco's *View of Toledo* or, from the modernist standpoint, Picasso's *Guernica*.

The Chicago police had set up a barricade on the Inner Drive, enabling us to witness the brutal conclusion of the first Day of Rage. By turning on the TV, I had the additional benefit of being able to watch the proceedings in stereo. Renzler, of course, got to experience it in quad.

It seemed almost impossible to keep in perspective that we were there for an entirely different purpose, for the spectacle we witnessed made Sherri West's kidnapping seem mundane by comparison. But the condition of Reverend Whitey Howard and the untimely demise of Bill Walters were themselves sobering thoughts. It seemed like those events had taken place days ago. Besides, that is the purpose of this narration and there were a few details I had uncovered earlier in the evening that warranted my consideration. I share them with you now.

After dropping Renzler off at Cindi West's apartment, I continued on to Eden with the intention of searching Arnie Long's office for anything that might indicate or clarify his role in the entire escapade. We were disinclined to suspect Arnie of anything other than congenital stupidity, but his quick exit during our meeting that evening and the subsequent death of Bill Walters gave us reason to wonder if our presumption of innocence had not been premature.

Breaking into young Long's office was not the sort of task one performs with muscle and crowbar. It was a finesse job, a piece of work hand-carved for Renzler, not really suitable for a lumbering fellow like myself. So I enlisted the aid of Marla and Mindi, who had access to the key, and conducted the search while Marla stood sentry outside the door and Mindi sat *shiva* at the entrance to Eden.

Arnie had not returned home since his sudden departure, a fact that struck me as peculiar if he had been involved in the killing of Walters. I expected he would want to establish an alibi for himself. His absence did not absolve him of suspicion, however, because there might have been some other matters for him to attend to. In addition, he might have been busy establishing an alibi somewhere else. Perhaps at the Paradise Room, where he would be instantly recognized, and, from what we had been able to gather, remembered, because it sounded as if he was universally loathed.

My search turned up nothing to directly implicate the lad. No scrawled notes with Walters' address, no appointments with Cindi West or Pablo Johnson recorded. But I didn't expect to find any such thing, thinking that even Arnie would have the sense to be scrupulously careful about revealing himself. In fact, I entered his office with no idea what it was that I was looking for. I knew only that I would know it when I found it, if there was anything to find.

In checking his calendar, I did not see any mention of a dinner meeting with Faith Wyder, although there were lunch and dinner dates listed with numerous other people. I wondered if this was an oversight on his part or if he had deliberately concealed it. As unlikely as it seemed that Arnie was part of a plot to extort money from his own father, it seemed even more unlikely that he would conspire with the daughter of Len Wyder to the same end.

But as Renzler occasionally says when he's drunk or feeling philosophical: "Nothing surprises me except surprise itself." I tell you, that boy's got poetry in him.

I discovered that Arnie had been keeping files on all the principals in the case—Pablo Johnson, Cindi and Sherri West, Whitey Howard, the Wyders and Walters. But there was nothing in any of them that indicated Arnie knew more than he was saying. And nothing of any interest, save for some truly maudlin love letters penned by Cindi West, followed by some truly nasty hate letters crayoned by Cindi West.

Arnie even had a file on Renzler, which had yours truly recorded in parentheses. If I uncovered anything to implicate him, the boy would never outlive his regrets about thinking of me as a mere afterthought. The file was thin and included some notes that Arnie had scrawled about my detective friend, most likely after one of their recent phone conversations.

I share them with you for their entertainment value: "Abrasive, haughty, sarcastic, condescending. Bad manners, bad attitude."

Yes, indeed, that's my friend Renzler, all right. Young Long was a keen judge of character.

One of the more interesting things I found in Arnie's drawers was a collection of pornography. This was not the sort of material that Arnie and his father were in the business of peddling, mind you. It was some truly scurrilous stuff, all the more remarkable because it was in the possession—and carefully hidden in his bottom drawer—of the only son of one of the world's most notable playboys.

I got the distinct impression that Arnie Long harbored a distinct sexual preference for members of the same sex.

I felt a little guilty for having peered into the young man's secret life, especially because I was beginning to think that there was no reason for having violated his privacy. But then I found something that made me feel totally absolved of any impropriety—something that Renzler would no doubt find extremely interesting if he ever returned to earth.

It was right in his top drawer, though not in plain sight. I should point out that I have seen art galleries in New York that take up less space than Arnie's desk.

I discovered that Arnie Long was planning on taking a vacation to Acapulco. This is a reasonable urge for a wealthy young man with no apparent full-time job during the fall or winter in a city as criminally cold as Chicago. But the fact that he was planning to leave the day after Faith Wyder was scheduled to deliver a suitcase full of money to an unknown party gave me cause for some degree of wonderment. And there was not one plane ticket but two, and the return flight was ticketed as "open."

Perhaps Arnie, unlike me, was one of those seasoned flyers who think nothing of calling on the day of their departure to make a reservation. Or perhaps Arnie was planning on taking a very long vacation, no pun intended.

But I think it was the name on the second ticket that intrigued me more than anything else. The last name was Walker, and instead of a first name there was only the initial F.

I returned my attention to Arnie Long's desk calendar and began looking more carefully at his recent dates. In going back through the previous four weeks, I found F. Walker listed six times. Two of the dates were dinner appointments, the other four were not specified. On one other day I found a listing for F. W., and I wondered how I could have possibly overlooked it during my first examination. That was the sort of detail that Renzler never would have missed.

As I flipped back to the date that really interested me, I knew what I would find even before I got there. For the night of the Friday when Renzler had found Sherri West with Steve Farrell, the night on which he and I had taken the girls out for the prime of their life and Arnie Long had been dining with Faith Wyder, his calendar indicated that he had an appointment with F. Walker.

My friend Renzler says that I have an inclination to jump to conclusions, but I did not think I was jumping on this occasion. It appeared to this amateur detective that Faith and Arnie were planning on taking a long walk together.

It occurred to me then that I should accidentally on purpose remove the tickets from Arnie's desk. But thinking that knowledge is power, I decided to leave them there so as not to arouse Arnie's suspicion and talk over my findings with Renzler when he returned from Cindi West's apartment later that evening. Of course, at that time I had no idea what kind of condition Renzler would be in when he got back from that outing.

As I watched the reflection of the sun rising above the waters of Lake Michigan on Thursday at dawn, I decided it was finally time to attempt to discuss the matter with Brother Renzler. Despite a rather lengthy and dramatic monologue in which he reenacted his career-ending baseball injury, he had been showing signs of increasing coherence over the last hour or so.

I'm sorry to report that I misjudged the speed of his recovery. The resolution of an LSD trip—coming down, if you will—is often punctuated with periods of clarity. Eventually, the length of the punctuation will exceed the duration and intensity of the psychedelic episodes.

But Renzler was not quite there yet.

Rather than discuss the case with him, I ended up listening to a very funny story about the time he and his first wife, Amy, had been evicted from their apartment on the West Side of Manhattan. I had heard the story before, but on that occasion Amy was actually there in the room. On this occasion Renzler only *thought* she was there. I laughed along with my friend, but in all honesty I think I enjoyed the first version more. There was a meeting scheduled in four hours that it would be wise for us to attend. One hour after that, there was another meeting. Attendance at that one would be mandatory.

For the next hour or so, I attempted to broach the subject of business whenever the opportunity presented itself. At one point, Renzler nodded and said, "The case. You're right, Nate. We have to discuss the case."

I narrated, for the third time, the account of my search of Arnie Long's office. That was followed by a long moment of silence, which in turn was followed by this:

"I've figured it out, Nate. I've figured the whole thing out." He was pacing the room with a cigarette in one hand and a beer in the other.

"Great," I urged him on, thinking perhaps that he had finally returned to a perspective in the vicinity of reality. "What do you think the answer is?"

He fell silent for a short period of time, during which he appeared to be concentrating. At last he smiled and said, "I forgot. I completely forgot what we were talking about."

I closed my eyes and groaned, then got up and walked to the table, where I had left my stash of amphetamines. I took one with a beer and tried to determine what I should do regarding my suspicions about Arnie Long. It appeared that I was going to be in charge of directing the day's production, which would have been fine with me if it were only a movie.

I sat down and tried to visualize the set—Lincoln Park decorated with cops for props and crawling with bad actors. The second day of four Days of Rage. It was enough to make a forty-six-year-old man who had stayed up all night tired and cranky.

At 9 A.M., I picked up the phone and canceled Arnie Long's plane reservations.

CHAPTER 26

Renzler's condition had improved considerably by the time we showered, dressed, summoned the car and began driving to Eden for our meeting with the motley crew, minus one. William Walters, public relations genius and amateur shakedown artist, would be unable to attend. Although Renzler had developed an inexplicable fondness for the fellow, I did not feel any inclination to grieve. It was not as if I actually felt happy he was dead, only that his passing did not produce any drain on my emotional reservoir.

I was spared the trouble of calling the police, as Renzler would have done, to ascertain the cause of Walters' death. I was quite relieved, because this sort of task confuses me to distraction. In addition, the police are about as cooperative as Catholic girls on a first date when it comes to disseminating information to private detectives. Fortunately, toward the back of that morning's newspaper, beyond the banner headlines and photos of the war we had witnessed the night before, I found a short account of the apparent suicide.

I say suicide because that was the suspicion raised by the police in the newspaper report. I add apparent because there was no conclusive determination offered and no mention of a suicide note. I didn't know if this point was an oversight on the part of the reporter or a blunder on the part of Walters' killer, assuming that the killer wanted it to look like suicide. If there was a note, I would be curious to see it. I would be interested in finding out if the handwriting bore any resemblance to some that I had seen in recent weeks, particularly that of Arnie Long.

The newspaper story did contain eyewitness testimony from one Hillary Mathieson, seventy-three, who said, "I was looking up and all of a sudden he just jumped. Just like that." You could be sure newspaper sales increased significantly that day on account of multiple purchases by Hillary and her legions of friends.

On a slower news day, I am sure, the story would have contained quotes from Walters' associates and friends, perhaps a pair of carefully crafted platitudes about the world's great loss from Walters' two most recent employers. But as I understand it, releasing those kinds of statements is the responsibility of the PR director, and he obviously was not available for comment. So let the record show that Bill Walters' obituary ran without a photograph.

Of course, I had not the slightest interest in seeing a photo of the man. The only part of the story that held any real interest for me was a sentence near the end: "Police said traces of alcohol were found in Mr. Walters' blood, but there was no sign that he had taken any drugs."

In the detective business, that is what we call a clue. Unless Pablo Johnson had altered his modus operandi—and he certainly had not in the case of Renzler later that evening—someone other than Pablo had pushed Bill Walters out of his apartment window.

Renzler was feeling so sprightly by the time we got started that he insisted on doing the driving. This suggestion met with stubborn resistance from yours truly. To humor my friend, I permitted him to settle the dispute in our customary fashion, which is to flip a coin. All the while, I was prepared to find another excuse if his luck, which is usually execrable, turned out to be good.

When, after flipping the coin, he made the determination that it had two heads and no tails, we both agreed that he would be better suited to riding in the passenger seat. But since he was not entirely incoherent by this time, I took the opportunity to repeat my report on Arnie Long and disclose to him the newspaper details regarding the death of Walters.

He remained silent throughout, nodding assuredly at certain points. This gave me some hope that he would have some thoughts on how to proceed. But when I reached the conclusion, he began to imitate Chuck Thompson, the baseball broadcaster for the Baltimore Orioles, announcing a Brooks Robinson grand-slam home run to win the fourth and final game of the World Series.

I see no reason to go into any detail about how the real Series differed from the one played in the ballpark of Renzler's mind. Suffice it to say that he lost a considerable amount of money and was forced to avoid all of his neighborhood bars for months following the Mets' victory. But as I listened to his booming play-by-play, I got an awful, sinking feeling in my gut.

I don't like going to the racetrack or playing poker, because I am overcome with inertia brought on by pathological ambivalence. Today I would be playing in a high-stakes game, with full responsibility for calling all the shots. After a night without sleep, in the midst of a speed crash and on an empty stomach, no less.

As we turned off Lake Shore Drive at Fullerton—I had decided to boycott the park until our presence was absolutely essential—I began to mull possible strategies for confronting young Arnie Long with my suspicions. But by the time we entered Eden, I still had not formulated any conclusions, except to follow Renzler's guidelines in situations of doubt: "When you don't know how to play it, play it by ear." The last time I had relied on this methodology, I lost $500 at Aqueduct.

Alas, my friend has better ears than I do. He won $200 that day.

I was glad to see the girls before we had to face the clients, and they seemed genuinely glad to see us. Renzler, still on cloud nine after winning all his World Series bets, would have been glad to see a poodle pissing on his foot. It seemed small consolation that my friend was maintaining a predominantly happy demeanor instead of becoming morose.

Naturally, the girls wanted to know all the details of Renzler's trip, and while it would have been far more pleasurable to recount them than to continue to our meeting, I felt forced to remind them that we had business to attend to first. Had I been more at ease, I would have thought to suggest that they read all about it in my chapters when the book goes on sale.

"They're all here," Mindi said. "They're waiting for you in the Sanctuary. It's really creepy quiet in there."

"We better hurry," I said, disengaging Renzler from an embrace with his young squeeze.

"Don't worry, Nate," he answered. "You can count on me. My battery's recharged. I'm ready."

If only I could have believed him.

Arnie Long was apparently ready as well, or perhaps the silence in the Sanctuary had become too much for him to bear. He met us halfway down the hall, addressing Renzler first, because after all, I am merely a man living in parentheses.

Although I hadn't planned my confrontation with the lad, it suddenly became clear that this was my opportunity to play it by ear. Launching into an accusation with his father and the odious competition present could prove to be a mistake. The ideal circumstance would be to have Miss Wyder present as well, but we detectives rarely work in the realm of the ideal.

As Arnie Long strutted toward us in his ever-officious gait, I became aware of how I was going to play it—naturally, and with hostility. Rather like a Bach fugue.

"We've been waiting for you," he said to Renzler. "Did you hear about Bill Walters?"

Renzler nodded. "Yes, Arnie, we're on the job. Aren't we, Nate?"

"What do you think? The newspaper said it was suicide."

Suddenly, it struck me as peculiar that Arnie hadn't called on the phone when he heard about Walters' death. I wondered if he had decided to avoid Renzler intentionally or perhaps didn't call because he knew Renzler would be in no condition to talk.

"You can't believe everything you read in the newspaper," Renzler answered. His reply appeared to leave young Long a bit unsatisfied.

"Mr. Renzler had a little accident last night," I said. "An asshole named Pablo Johnson tried to stuff him full of LSD."

"Good Christ!" Arnie seemed surprised, but I was not going to be misled by possible dramatic acting skills gleaned in a college theater arts class.

"He's OK now," I said. "But it's been a rather long night, and he's still a bit foggy."

"No, no, I'm fine," Renzler said. "Feel like a hundred bucks."

"Perhaps I can answer your questions about Walters," I suggested. "Yes, we heard about it. No, it was not suicide. It was murder."

An "oh gosh" look spread over Arnie's face, then he said, "Well, I suppose he deserved it. I guess the kidnappers must have killed him to shut him up. You didn't get a chance to talk to him, did you?"

"No," I said, "we didn't. If we had, we would have called to tell you about it. We were even a little surprised not to hear from you." I paused to let that sink in, then added, "We think someone named F. Walker is involved in the killing."

It would have taken years of acting lessons for Arnie to perform his way out of that scene. Even in the dim light of the hallway, the panic on his face was easier to read than an article in *Reader's Digest*. He was as naked and exposed as Michelangelo's *David*, the only difference being that David wasn't clutching his nuts like someone had just kicked them.

Following a few precious moments of speechlessness, he managed to stammer, "I was very busy last night, and I didn't hear about Walters until this morning." And then back on the offensive: "And it seems like every time I call Renzler, it seems like I'm interrupting him."

I paused for a moment to let Renzler respond, but he seemed to be waiting for me. I had a feeling that despite the acid, he had a relatively good sense of what was going on. Being aware of his condition, he was content to let me do the work.

I resumed with one of his tactics—adopt an understanding tone, then stick it in the gut.

"Relax, Arnie, don't worry about it," I said. "I'm sure you've had a lot on your mind with the kidnapping and all. We're certainly not annoyed that you didn't call. After all, we're the ones who are working for you."

He nodded appreciatively and motioned down the hall. "We should move on," he said. "Dad's waiting."

"Sure," I replied, beginning to walk beside him. "But we were hoping you might be able to help. You know Walters. We thought maybe you might know this guy Walker."

Arnie shook his head and continued walking. I touched his shoulder for emphasis. A light touch, nothing threatening. Just enough to make him stop and look at me.

"Or maybe Walker's not a guy," I said.

Arnie avoided my glance and looked at Renzler. Renzler was looking at me. There was definitely a sense of recognition beneath that acid glaze.

Arnie shrugged and shook his head. You could hear him swallow in the silence. "No," he said, beginning to walk again. "I've never heard the name."

"Well, maybe your father has," I said. We were nearing the Sanctuary.

"No, he hasn't. I'm sure he hasn't."

"Well, maybe I'll ask him—you know, just in case."

CHAPTER 27

My inquisition of Arnie Long gave me additional confidence for when we entered the Sanctuary. The girls were not permitted entry on this occasion, but before leaving, Mindi said that she had something important to tell me. From previous conversations, I had learned that Mindi's urgency meter had a more extensive range than mine, but this time I got the distinct impression that she was not inclined to unburden her mind in the presence of Arnie. I promised to speak with her at my first opportunity.

The room was indeed deadly silent—"creepy quiet," if you prefer Mindi's way with words. They were seated at a long table, larger than the one depicted in Ghirlandaio's version of the *Last Supper*, if that gives you any frame of reference. It was covered with a predominantly white table cloth festooned with fig leaves and serpents of varying hues. And although I felt as if we might soon be facing the prospect of a modern-day crucifixion, it was clear that Arnold Long had something different in mind—not bread and wine but steak and eggs, not the last supper but the ultimate brunch.

The amphetamines had annihilated my usually hearty appetite, but wisdom dictated that I force myself to consume some of the offerings. It was likely that Renzler also would feel no inclination to partake, but I would make sure that a few of the essential vitamins and minerals made their way into his system.

Len Wyder sat at one end of the table, his rival at the other. Faith, looking ever so prim and proper in a black leather jumpsuit, was sitting immediately to her father's left. As soon as we entered, Arnie walked to the Long end of the table and stood at the right hand of his father.

"Pablo Johnson tried to give Renzler an overdose of LSD last night," he announced.

"What?" Arnold Long let out the first gasp, just a split second ahead of Len Wyder.

"What the lad sayeth be true," I answered. "Sherri was being held captive at her sister's apartment. Renzler got inside, but Johnson slugged him from behind. They slipped him some of the acid, but he managed to escape."

"What about Sherri? Did he get Sherri?"

I began to answer Arnold Long's question, but Wyder interrupted me with one of his own. "Where were you when all this was going on?"

"Gentlemen, gentlemen, one question at a time, please." Any anxiety that I had felt about the meeting was rapidly dissipating, giving way to a strong sense of distaste for everyone in the room. Save myself and Renzler, of course. "And time is something we don't have much of," I added, taking a seat in the middle of the table alongside my friend.

"Sherri attempted to escape as well," I said to Arnold Long, "but Johnson was apparently able to recapture her. Johnson tied Renzler's hands behind his back, so there wasn't much he could do. When I went back there a few hours later, the apartment was empty."

I looked at Wyder. "As for where I was when all this was going on, I happened to be at the scene of a murder. You've no doubt heard that Bill Walters was pushed out a window last night."

"Yeah, of course I heard about it," Wyder said. "But the newspaper said it was suicide."

"Surely you jest," I answered.

Renzler let out a snort that indicated his recovery was proceeding. "You can't be that naive," he said.

"Of course it was murder," Arnold Long said. "Any idiot could have figured that out."

"Who are you callin' an idiot, asshole?"

"Shut up, goddamnit." If I couldn't dazzle them with verbiage, I could certainly intimidate them with volume.

"The little weasel had it coming to him," Faith Wyder grumbled through a truckload of scrambled eggs. "I'm just sorry I didn't get the chance to break the little worm's neck in my bare hands."

"I don't think there's much question that Walters' loss is the world's gain," I replied. "But it's your loss, too, because we didn't get a chance to talk to him."

"Hey, that's right," her father said. "Do you got my money?"

I had been considering holding Wyder's payoff to Walters as a deposit against our fee. But that seemed perhaps too hostile a gesture even to me, so I pulled it out of my jacket pocket and tossed it onto the table. I did, however, make a point of returning Arnold Long's stack of bills first.

"Here it is, Len," I said. "Now—where's the ransom money?"

Wyder pointed to a small pink suitcase in a corner of the room that was approximately equidistant from him and Arnold Long. I wondered if they had managed to agree on a mutually suitable location without an altercation.

"The suitcase belongs to Faith," Wyder said, apparently a caution against anyone who might be harboring notions of stealing it. "My bills are all marked. He didn't bother to mark his."

"That's right," Arnold Long said. "I didn't see any reason for it."

I stifled a modest urge to chuckle over Long's response, but his son was unable to follow my example of restraint. I thought perhaps he was loosening up a bit over my failure to mention F. Walker in connection with Walters' murder. I had decided to save that surprise for later.

"What's so funny, Junior?" Wyder demanded, rising halfway out of his chair.

"Your face," Arnie retorted.

Hardly the material for a guest spot on "The Tonight Show,"

but Arnie's dad laughed appreciatively. This so incensed Wyder that he reached for a handful of hash browns.

"Throw it and die," I warned, pointing a finger for effect. I did not object as much to his intention of hurling the food as I did to the likelihood that he would misfire and hit Renzler or myself.

For a moment I thought he was going to test my threat, but he reconsidered and dropped his fat ass back into the seat, dumping the potatoes disgustedly onto his plate. Faith had been poised at the ready with her fork, but I restrained her with a cautioning stare.

"OK, listen up, here's the plan," I said, thinking to myself that I sounded exactly like my high school football coach did when he had no idea what play to run. "Faith will carry the suitcase. Renzler, Arnie and I will follow."

"Why does Arnie have to go with you?" Apparently, Dad was concerned about the boy's safety.

"Because I want him to," I answered. That seemed sufficient explanation for Arnold, although my real reason was to ensure that his son wouldn't get any ideas about wandering out of the big picture while we were gone.

"What about Renzler? Is he in any condition to go?" Now it was Arnie raising the questions, perhaps thinking that it might be easier to escape if only one of us were watching him.

"I'm fine," Renzler assured him. "I just love going to the zoo."

"You two will wait for us back here," I said to Long and Wyder.

"Why do I gotta stay here?"

"Because I said so." Up to that point, I hadn't really considered the possibility that Len Wyder might be involved in the kidnapping of Sherri West. Certainly not with the joint participation of Arnie Long. But he was a greedy man, and greedy men have been known to do surprisingly greedy things. I recalled Renzler's position vis-à-vis surprises: "Nothing surprises me except surprise itself."

Wyder stood up. "No way. I brought the money. I ate his lousy food. My part's finished. Now I'm going back to my own house."

"Your part's not finished," I corrected him. "It's only just beginning. Because when we get back from the park, whatever happens, we're going to reassemble here and discuss Bill Walters' murder. There's at least one person in this room who knows more about it than he's saying. Maybe there are two, maybe there are four."

"What? You're crazy!" Arnold Long was standing now, the brunch officially concluded. "Talk to this guy, Renzler," he pleaded. "He's not making any sense."

Renzler shrugged. "I don't know, Arnold. He's making sense to me."

Long wheeled and faced his son. "Do you know what he's talking about, Arnie?"

The son feigned bewilderment. "I haven't the slightest idea, Dad."

"You'll find out soon enough," I said. "Until then, you"—I pointed at Wyder—"are confined to quarters. If you jump ship, I'll find you and throw you overboard." The amphetamines were really making the old ticker pump now. "That goes for everybody. Anyone who isn't here when we get back from the park will be considered guilty until proven innocent."

"That's ridiculous," Arnold Long shouted. His son and the Wyders were clearly in agreement with him, perhaps for the first time ever. Or perhaps for the second time ever.

"I'm sorry, Mr. Long," I said, thinking that I might have overplayed the heavy role somewhat. "But that's the way it has to be."

It was apparent from his silence that Arnold was not entirely convinced. I picked up the suitcase and handed it to Faith. As the four of us filed out of the room, I could hear Arnold Long and Len Wyder jabbering away.

"Do you have a sense of what's going on yet?" I asked Renzler as we walked down the hall.

"Yeah, I do," he said. "I'm just thinking a little slowly, that's all. You did a good job in there."

I felt a momentary surge of pride, almost like getting a pat on the ass from Coach Wackowicz for making a game-saving tackle. Then Renzler added, "Is this Wednesday or Thursday?"

CHAPTER 28

The breeze from Lake Michigan was swirling the leaves around us as we began the trek to the zoo. The sun, which had been hidden behind the clouds a couple of hours before, had decided to make a prominent appearance after all. The result was what you and I might call perfect football weather. Or, invoking the memory of Coach one last time, pussy weather.

As I walked beside Renzler and behind Arnie and Faith, who had opted for single file, I felt like we were on a team that was certain to get its butt kicked. This gave us something in common with the weathermen and other militants, whose ranks had dwindled after the previous night's casualties and who were clearly outnumbered by the cops. The latter, in turn, looked rather eager to get on with the game.

It was a very short walk from Eden to the site for the drop, but I directed the kiddies south along Lincoln Park West before actually going into the park. If we had turned on Fullerton and taken the most direct route to the bird house, there was no doubt that Johnson and his associates would spot us right away. The notes had warned against shadowing Faith Wyder, and while Renzler had told me that he had no intention of following the instructions to the letter, I saw no good reason for being obvious about breaking them.

We conducted our trip virtually in silence, except for a few feeble attempts by yours truly to generate a bit of conversation.

Actually, conversation was not what I had in mind. My intention was to make Arnie and Faith as uncomfortable as possible.

"Have you two had dinner together lately?" I asked.

Arnie stared straight ahead and continued walking, but Faith looked askance over her shoulder.

"I don't think they're in a very good mood," Renzler said, with sufficient volume for them to hear. When his attention span permitted, my friend was becoming capable of accurate observation.

"Hey, Faith," I called, "do you think we'll see F. Walker in the park?"

This question halted her forward progress temporarily, causing Arnie to stop also. But when she turned to face me, her reaction was one of incomprehension.

"What?" Even on words of one syllable, her voice had the timbre of a stopping car that was badly in need of new brake shoes.

"You're not acquainted with F. Walker? I thought the name might be something that you and Arnie had in common."

"I told you I don't know who you're talking about." Arnie was capable of being very prissy on some occasions. This was one of them.

"Do you mean Fred Walker?"

There was always the possibility that Faith had risen to the occasion of spontaneous fabrication, but her tone belied a sense of authentic bewilderment.

"I don't know the first name," I said. "Perhaps Arnie can help us out."

Au contraire, Arnie did not provide any help. Did not even attempt to muster another denial, save for an irritated sigh.

"Do you know who's he talking about?" Faith asked him.

"No, he's crazy. The man's insane," Arnie replied, without bothering to correct her grammar.

Faith smiled at me, revealing traces of scrambled eggs that were still waiting to be digested. "Maybe so," she said. "But I kinda like him, anyway."

Renzler elbowed me and spoke in a lowered voice. "That's the ultimate compliment, partner. If I were you, I'd run with it."

"Indeed. Maybe I should just run."

As we reached the corner of Dickens, I decided not to pursue the matter any further. I had partially succeeded in accomplishing what I set out to do; namely, upset Arnie. If he was a conspirator in the plot, he was going to be an anxious one at the least. Faith, on the other hand, had proven to be completely unflappable. Almost too much so, it seemed to me. But then I was something of a nerve case myself, attributable to insufficient sleep, more than sufficient speed and extenuating circumstances.

We stood at the edge of the park for a few moments and surveyed the landscape. There may not have been enough protestors to launch a revolution, but there were plenty to provide cover for a guerrilla operation. They were roaming freely about, apparently having chosen to postpone the combat for later in the day. Or perhaps Mark Rudd had given them the afternoon off. For the moment, they were conducting themselves as normal people might—lounging under trees, throwing Frisbees, visiting the zoo.

The weather being pleasant, the scene looked almost like a slice of Americana cut straight out of Norman Rockwell's pie-eyed imagination. Given Norman's technical skill and hearty optimism, I'm sure he would have figured a way to leave the cops out of the picture.

The park slopes down slightly from Lincoln Park West, where we were standing, then levels off about fifty yards east at another street that runs north through it. After you cross that street, the zoo entrance is approximately 200 yards north and to the east. The bird house is at the north end of the zoo, no more than a three-minute walk along the winding pathways past the other buildings and cages. On a day when the park was not crowded, it was conceivable that it might be possible to see someone across the way at the zoo entrance from close to where we were situated. At the moment, however, it was impossible to conceive of a day when the park was not crowded.

"Do you have any thoughts?" I asked Renzler.

"Only impure ones," he answered. "How about you?"

"I think we better stick real close to her—twenty-five yards, fifty at the most."

"We could split up," he said.

I looked at the cops stationed around the park watching the crowd, then looked at Renzler watching the crowd through the $1.98 sunglasses he had purchased at a rest station on the New Jersey Turnpike.

"You remember what happened to you the last time we split up," I said.

"Yeah, and I remember what happened the last time I tried to flip a coin."

"OK, you can start walking," I instructed Faith. "But bear in mind that you're not in any hurry. I want you to walk real slowly, like you were about to receive your first Holy Communion."

"Sure, big guy. I'll do whatever you say. Besides, it's hard to walk fast in this outfit. The leather is just *gripping* at my flesh."

"Uh-huh," Renzler said as she began to strut down the hill.

"And don't look behind you," I called after her. She nodded without turning around, proving to be more attentive than I expected.

"If we don't stand out like sore thumbs in this crowd, she certainly will," Arnie said. "I think Renzler's right. Maybe we should split up."

Renzler answered him before I could formulate a suitably sarcastic reply. "It's all for one and one for all," he said. "Besides, if you walk like you've got a broomstick up your ass, they'll probably think you're a cop."

I thought a nearby cop might have overheard my friend's remark, so I began to move us along. The last thing I desired at that moment was an encounter with the Chicago police, even if we did look more like them than us.

Faith was following my instructions as literally as a creationist interprets the Bible. We had to pause at the bottom of the hill to permit her a longer lead. From that point to the zoo entrance it was a flat, wide-open field. Once she reached the winding pathways inside the zoo, it would be necessary to shorten the gap.

In the initial stages, there was no difficulty following her, despite the clusters of people blocking our view. Arnie Long proved to be correct in his assertion that she stood out in the crowd. Although she hardly warranted a second glance after the benefit of a close-up look, from a distance in her hooker ensemble she was attracting more stares than shit draws flies. If we did happen to lose sight of her, all we needed to do was follow the gazes of horny young men.

I was beginning to get a sense of optimism, which is quite rare for me, being a keen believer in Murphy's Law—if it can go wrong, it will. But as we were crossing into the open field, the law suddenly took effect in the form of someone yelling, "Hey, Renzler, Mark Renzler," to the south of us.

I turned to see an overweight, balding man about twenty yards away. He was staggering toward us in a maniacal sprint that resembled the Australian crawl, if you can imagine that stroke being attempted on dry land.

I failed to notice his pony tail until just about the time Renzler, in the throes of recognition, said, "Jesus Christ, it's Moses Godley." There was a sense of happiness in my friend's voice that could only be attributable to residual traces of acid still circulating through his system.

On another occasion, I might have answered, "My name is not Jesus Christ," but instead I turned around to make sure Faith Wyder was still in range of our radar. I had no difficulty spotting the object of park vagrants' unrequited lust, but she was probably fifty yards away. It might have been my imagination, but from that distance, she appeared to be walking at a quicker pace now.

"We've got to hurry," I told Renzler.

He nodded. "Don't worry, Nate. This will only take a second."

By the time he reached us, more than a second later, Godley was huffing and puffing like an asthmatic octogenarian who has just finished blowing out the candles on his birthday cake. I would guess that he was thirty years away from that event, but still far enough along to induce a coronary with a modicum of exertion. When the blood finally drained from his face, I noticed that he bore a haunting resemblance to someone I had met recently, although I could not for the life of me remember exactly who it was.

"You made it!" he said, gasping for breath and pumping Renzler's hand as if they were long-lost brothers.

"Yeah, we made it," Renzler said, grinning. My friend, the revolutionary.

"It was hell last night, Mark, sheer hell. The pigs were fucking murderous."

"I know," Renzler answered. "We watched the end of it from our hotel window."

"Excuse me, we've got to go," I said. I looked at Arnie, who was gazing off toward Faith Wyder, and wondered if it was anxiety or hopefulness that I saw in his face.

"Yeah, that's right, we're in a hurry," Renzler said.

"Hey, did you see Pablo?" Godley asked.

Renzler reacted to the question with a slightly bewildered expression on his face. I hoped he would have the good sense not to attempt a recollection of his encounter with Johnson the night before.

"You mean last night, in the march?" he asked.

"No, man, *today*," Godley replied. "He's *here*, man, in the park. I saw him. Just a few minutes ago. He saw me and took off. A guy I talked to just back there said he passed him up near the conservatory." Godley pointed north, past a sprawling series of flower beds that lay beyond the entrance to the zoo.

I immediately put my hand on Renzler's arm. One of the most powerful properties—perhaps *the* most powerful—of LSD is its suggestive effect. A person under the influence of the drug may be in such a highly suggestible state that merely being asked if he needs to urinate will make him feel an urgent need to do so. As I watched Renzler turn and scan the crowded field of hippies, many of whom bore at least a vague resemblance to Pablo Johnson, I was certain that he probably saw ten or more facsimiles of the dreaded creature.

Even if Johnson was loitering in the park, our primary concern at the moment had to be following Faith Wyder. Or at least that was my view of the options before us. Renzler might have disagreed, of course, and if he were in a more operable condition, I would have gone along with his judgment.

At this point, I was becoming so overwhelmed with panic that I cannot recall for certain who spoke next. I can remember Godley saying that he would cherish the opportunity to get his hands around Johnson's neck and Renzler responding to that with enthusiastic affirmation.

I remember tugging at Renzler's arm and saying, "Come on, we've got to get moving." And I remember thinking that I had shaken him out of his reverie when he nodded and turned back toward me.

But suddenly, Godley, with piss-poor timing, issued the suggestion that made Renzler feel like he was about to wet his pants.

"I see him!" he shouted. "Up there! He's wearing a blue jacket! He's going into the conservatory!"

"Yeah, you're right, there he is," Renzler yelled. He pulled away from me and started to bolt across the field.

I wheeled and in the distance saw Faith Wyder entering the zoo, at which time I entered into a crisis of emotional conflict. My sense of professionalism dictated that I should continue following her. My sense of friendship dictated that I should follow Renzler. A classic moment in the annals of ambivalence involving a walking classic textbook example of the dreaded affliction.

What is professionalism but a job? I thought. *What is a job but servitude in the pursuit of money?*

Renzler is an adult who can take care of himself, I thought. *Renzler is a thirty-eight-year-old child who's tripping his brains out.*

"Follow her," I ordered Arnie Long. "Don't lose sight of her. If I don't catch up with you here in the park, go immediately back to your father's place and wait for me. Make sure Faith goes back there, too. Understand?"

I do believe I scared the living daylights out of the boy. People tell me I can be rather intimidating when I raise my voice.

He recoiled, then nodded in a manner that seemed almost a salute. As he began walking, I added, "If you don't show up back at the house, Arnie, I'm going to find you and break every bone in your body."

I spoke now to Moses Godley, who had observed my tantrum with understandable incredulity. "Come on, fatso," I said. "It was your dumb idea to chase Johnson in the first place."

I knew when I started out that I had not a prayer of catching up with Renzler until he decided to stop running. The man is a living testament to fitness through vice. He smokes at least twice as many cigarettes as I do, and he can run at least twice as fast. While I don't necessarily follow a regular program of exercise, I do stop by the gym once a week to punch the light bag and have a few beers. Renzler, by contrast, has probably seen a confessional more recently than he's seen a locker room, and I'm almost certain he has not stepped foot inside a church for five years.

In addition to his superior speed, he was 100 yards ahead of me when I began to run. Fortunately, he has considerable natural agility, so he was succeeding in threading his way through the crowd without any collisions. If he had long hair, a few of the cops would have undoubtedly begun to chase after him; likewise with me.

By the time I had negotiated the flower beds and reached the steps of the conservatory, I was in a condition that approximated that of Moses Godley a few minutes before. Before going inside, I turned to gauge one old man's progress against another's, but he seemed to have abandoned the pursuit in its early stages.

The conservatory was comprised of a series of greenhouses, the paths through which formed something of a minor labyrinthine jungle. A poster indicated that a chrysanthemum show was in progress, but it did not appear to be an especially big drawing card despite the free admission. While I harbor no doubts about their virility, I suspect that flower enthusiasts might have been inclined to avoid the park during the Days of Rage.

There were two main paths that forked at the entrance to the first room, apparently forming a somewhat elongated circle. Thinking that the natural inclination of a former second baseman turned ex-cop would be to take the path leading to the right, I veered left. As I began walking down the lush green corridor, it occurred to me that the conservatory might be a wonderful place to visit under the influence of powerful drugs.

This notion received substantial confirmation with my discovery of the solitary figure of Renzler standing in a small room at the rear of the conservatory, surrounded by mums and mumbling to himself. On the surface it was a scene worthy of Dante Gabriel Rossetti or one of the other Pre-Raphaelites, but given the circumstances, it was perhaps better suited to Salvador Dali.

"There's no smoking allowed in the conservatory, sir," I said.

He looked up and smiled at me, not even showing the decency to act startled. "I figured you probably went to the drop site," he said.

"You figured wrong."

"It's not the first time. Boy, oh, boy, did I ever screw things up."

"That's understating it a bit, if you don't mind my saying so."

"I don't mind. I think you're entitled to a few more of those before the score gets settled."

Despite his mad dash after the phantom Johnson and his tranquil reverie over the flowers, I had a sense that Renzler's recovery was proceeding rapidly now. I've been told that strenuous exertion can have that effect.

"Were the flowers talking back to you or was it strictly a one-way conversation?" I asked, exercising another one of my entitlements.

"Strictly one-way," he said. "And I wasn't talking to them. I was thinking out loud."

"Well I'm glad to hear you're thinking again, even if it does require moving your lips."

"Would you like to hear what I was thinking about or are you going to cash in all your IOUs now?"

"Might as well," I said, looking at my watch. "It's a little late to go to the bird house."

"But it's not too late to catch the person we're looking for," Renzler answered.

I suggested that would be better accomplished if we started moving, then asked him to elaborate on his recent thinking spree.

"I've decided that if you want to control the LSD, you can," he said. "But it takes a lot of concentration. For the last couple of minutes that's all I've been doing—concentrating. I think I'm in a state of control again. Once I realized that, I was able to think more clearly about things. I think maybe the LSD even helped me to think more clearly about things."

I thought perhaps my friend was getting a bit carried away, but he sounded sufficiently serious that it seemed like one of those rare moments when sarcasm is inappropriate. I merely asked, "Such as?"

"Such as the ransom note. There was a clue in it about the person knowing that we were working on the case. I think that clue might have been planted there deliberately to throw us off, to make us think that someone on the inside was behind the kidnapping."

"But there has to be someone on the inside, don't you think? Like the person who killed Bill Walters."

"Yeah, I think so. But that's not necessarily the person who killed Bill Walters. And that's definitely not the person who wrote the ransom note or the person who planned everything."

"There was another clue in the note, a phrase that sounded familiar to me. The note said Sherri West had 'great tits.' You wouldn't have known about it, because you weren't there when I heard him say it."

"I'm also the only person I know who hasn't seen Sherri West's tits," I reminded him.

"There's been a little too much coincidence for my taste. I think I've been overlooking someone all along."

"Someone who has a haunting resemblance to the Reverend Whitey Howard, perhaps?"

"Yeah, you noticed that, too."

"His younger brother, I would guess."

"Yeah, that sounds right," Renzler replied. "Pablo Johnson's uncle."

"If we drive fast, we can probably get back to his place before he does," I said, checking my watch.

"I'm feeling a lot better now," Renzler said. "Since I know the way, maybe it's a good idea for me to drive there."

"It's a terrible idea," I answered. "But if you act like a good boy and don't put up a fuss about it, I'll be a nice guy and let you start narrating again."

CHAPTER 29

Thanks to Nate's timely, if somewhat overblown, narration, you've now got a pretty good idea why I said Wednesday, October 8, was probably the longest day of my entire life.

And it wasn't over yet. Not by a long shot.

According to my definition, a day begins and ends with sleep. I could barely remember the last time I had gotten any. But I was damn sure it hadn't been in the last twenty-four hours.

It sounds ridiculous to say I was feeling refreshed by the time we got out of the conservatory and started walking up to the car. But adrenaline can make you feel that way, once you've got it pumping. Mine was going like a goddamn geyser.

Nate suggested that a small dose of amphetamines wouldn't hurt either. What the hell. Drugs were becoming part of my lifestyle. And it's tough to argue with a guy like Dr. Moore.

"I told Arnie to go back to Eden right away if I didn't find him in the park," Nate said. "But after the scene I made this morning, I'd prefer not to see Wyder and Arnold until we've got some good news for them. But I'd be curious to see if Arnie and Faith made it back, and I'm also wondering what the instructions were that were left at the drop site."

"I'm with you, partner. You're still calling the shots."

"Thanks for the vote of confidence. You know, I think this experience just might cure my ambivalence."

I shook my head. "There's only one cure for ambivalence."

"What's that?"

"Suicide."

"Hell, that won't work. I wouldn't be able to decide how to do it."

As we took a turn around a patch of trees on the path through the park, I saw Arnie Long and Faith Wyder walking side by side about 200 feet ahead of us. From a distance, they could have been two teenage kids on their way home from school. But I could see that Faith was toting her pink suitcase. I guess Arnie wasn't the sort who offered to carry a girl's books for her.

I made goddamn sure it wasn't a hallucination before I spoke up. "It looks like a couple of your worries have just been resolved," I said.

Nate shouted Arnie's name and they stopped in their tracks and turned. Seeing the pair of them standing there together reminded me of the two plane tickets that Nate told me were waiting back in Arnie's desk. It was a relief to find out that the drugs hadn't impaired my ability to recall important details. Unfortunately, I was also beginning to remember a few things that I'd just as soon forget.

When we got to about ten feet away, Arnie went into his moral outrage routine. "Where have you been?" he demanded. The question was addressed to Nate, so I let him field it.

"We went out to get a hot dog and a beer," he said. "What happened?"

"My father's going to be furious when he hears about how you messed this up. I don't see any reason why we should pay you." He was speaking to me now.

"We're pressed for time, Arnie," I said. "Just tell us what happened."

"He lost me," Faith said. "If I'da walked any slower, I woulda been picked up for street walkin'."

"Good work, Arnie," Nate said. "What about the instructions? Did you find them?"

"Yeah, they're right—"

"Good work!" Arnie's reaction time was slower than my third grade teacher's. But Sister Veronica had an excuse. She was eighty-three years old. "What about you? Running off after Renzler and leaving me to do the job I'm paying you to do? I told you he shouldn't have come with us."

I was tempted to deck the kid right there, but I knew I'd have a chance to do it sooner or later. I was hoping for sooner. As much as I disliked him, he did have a reasonable point. I had screwed things up. It was the unreasonable way he was making the point that bothered me.

"Put a lid on it," Nate shouted. He didn't bother to look up from the piece of paper Faith had handed to him.

"We're supposed to wait at his house till three o'clock," Faith said, pointing at Arnie. "Then we're supposed to get a phone call."

"It's quarter to one now," Nate said, checking his watch. "We've got a little over two hours."

I shook my head. "By that time he'll be long gone. Let's get going."

"What do we do about them?" He motioned toward Faith and Arnie.

I shrugged. "Send them home to their fathers."

"Hey, what's going on?" Arnie asked. We were beginning to walk away. "Where are you two going?"

"Out for another hot dog and beer," Nate called over his shoulder.

"Hey." This time it was Faith doing the squawking. It couldn't have been an easy task running in that jumpsuit, but she managed to catch up with us. "You're supposed to go back and wait for the phone call. That's what the instructions say."

"Don't worry. We'll be back in plenty of time," I said.

"And just what do you propose that we should do while you're gone?"

Nate shrugged. "You're planning a big trip tomorrow, right? Why don't you go home and start packing."

"What?" More outrage from Arnie. "How did you know about that?"

"I get voices in my head sometimes. One of the voices told me you'd be too busy, so I took the liberty of canceling your reservations."

"What?" With the blood rushing into Arnie's face, I could see the resemblance between him and his father. Up to that point, I thought maybe the mailman had been involved. "The nerve of you," he shouted. "You haven't heard the last of this."

Arnie turned on his heels and began to skulk toward Eden. "What about me?" Faith asked.

I smiled. "Why don't you keep an eye on Arnie."

"Remember what I said." Nate raised his voice to make sure Arnie could hear him. "If you're not there when we get back—you're dead."

CHAPTER 30

We left the children gazing vacantly into our car exhaust as we sped north toward Sheridan Road. We took a left at Belmont and then a right when we hit Clark. Four blocks up, we took a right onto Sheffield and parked in the first space we saw. We had the element of surprise in our favor, but we figured it was still smarter to go the rest of the way on foot.

It was 1 P.M. I was feeling almost clearheaded now, which is a rarity for me, even on good days.

Nate nodded when I told him. "That's the speed working," he said. "In a few hours you're going to feel like you got beat up by King Kong."

"Is there a drug to help that?"

"Yeah. Aspirin."

We headed west down an alley that ran behind the place. When we got to it, we had some decisions to make.

It was a two-story building. My guess was that he lived upstairs, but there was a basement, too. We tried to look into the two ground-level windows, but they were covered with a few decades' worth of city dirt and shut tighter than the lid on a new can of coffee.

I expected as much. He didn't strike me as the kind of guy who put a big investment into house cleaning.

We decided that Nate would wait on the back steps and I'd try to flush them out from the front. If he needed to get inside in a hurry, he could use the crowbar he had brought along for E-Z entry.

There was a CLOSED sign hanging on the door out front. Not one of those fancy, official-looking signs that you buy for seventy-nine cents in the hardware store, but a sheet of loose-leaf paper with some hasty dry-marker action on it. I had a feeling the sign was going to stay there until it was time for the city electrical inspector to come by for his next handout.

I looked in the window for evidence of life but didn't see any. I continued on to the far end of the building where there was another door, the one that led to the apartment upstairs. There was a lock on it that wouldn't have stood up to a strong gust of wind. Picking it was easier than getting drunk at a hockey game.

I counted a dozen stairs leading straight up. Then they took a sharp turn to the left. They were rotted and warped, just like you'd expect. I had to do a Rudolf Nureyev number to make sure they didn't creak.

As I began climbing, I started to wish I had been able to take my gun the night I escaped from Cindi's apartment. It suddenly dawned on me that it had only been last night. It felt like last week. There are times when a lot seems to happen in twenty-four hours. I had a feeling the next twenty-four were going to be proof of that.

When I reached the bend in the stairway, I could see a door at the top of the steps. I could hear muffled voices coming from behind it. I crept up the remaining four stairs and crouched down to listen in.

I could make out a male voice. It sounded different from the last time I heard it. Then it had been loud and cocky. This time it was whiny and scared. Pablo had given up Jimmy Cagney in favor of Elisha Cook, Jr.

"Come on, Uncle Bill, *please*. Just let us go. You can have all the money. I promise, I won't say anything."

"That's right." Cindi West's voice now. She sounded more shaky than Pablo. "We won't tell anybody. Just don't kill us."

Then Pablo again. "It doesn't serve any purpose." Ah, smart tactic, kid. Appeal to his sense of reason.

I tried to visualize the scene behind the door. Obviously, Uncle Bill had decided to cut Pablo and Cindi out of the deal. He had also decided to make sure it was the last deal they ever made. He must have been holding a gun on them. Maybe it was my gun. Maybe Pablo had gotten some ammunition for it and Uncle Bill had showed him how to load it. Then maybe Uncle Bill had decided to hold on to it for safekeeping.

Now I was really sorry I hadn't taken the gun. It would have been so much easier to march up the steps, fire a couple of rounds into the stairway wall and tell them to come out with their hands up. Of course, there was no reason to expect that anything would be easy.

I could tell from their voices that Pablo and Cindi were somewhere across the room, away from the door. So far, they'd been doing all the talking, so it was impossible to determine where old Uncle Bill was standing. To say nothing of Sherri, assuming she was in there with them.

I put my ear close to the door to listen for any little clue that would give Uncle Bill's location away. When one finally came, it startled me so much I almost fell down the goddamn stairs.

The telephone. It rang just in time to interrupt another one of Cindi's desperate pleas. Unless he had it wired to the stereo, the phone had to be right inside the door.

I heard footsteps coming toward me. Someone picked up the phone on the start of the third ring. Probably Uncle Bill, but I wasn't about to assume anything at that point.

"Hello." Uncle Bill, it was. "What? How long ago did they leave? What?"

It sounded to me like Mr. Inside had finally decided to call Mr. Outside. It had taken him (or her) a little longer than you might have expected. But maybe it took a while to figure out where Nate and I had gone. Or maybe there hadn't been a chance to get away to a phone.

So much for the element of surprise. But I was willing to trade it gladly for good information about Uncle Bill's present position. Of course, I had to make use of it fast. If he had any brains, the first thing he'd do when he got off the phone would be to open the door I was leaning against. Or at least go to the window to look outside. That would destroy any chance I had of getting a good crack at him.

I tested the door knob carefully while listening to Uncle Bill's outburst of exasperation.

"You idiot! Why didn't you call me sooner? Well, she's an idiot, too."

The door was unlocked. Maybe I was hitting a streak of good luck. I figured it was about time I got one.

"I'm not gonna listen to your stupid excuses. Too bad. I got my own problems to worry about."

I clutched the knob with my right hand across my body and leaned forward. I had to be ready to spring when the time was right. Chances were Uncle Bill had his back to the door so he could keep an eye on Pablo and Cindi.

"Are you sure they're coming here? Whaddaya mean, you don't know?"

I wondered if Nate could hear what was going on. By now, he'd be waiting at the back door. From seeing the first floor, I knew it couldn't be a very big apartment. My guess was that there was one more room before you hit the back entrance.

"Yeah, well fuck you, too!" Apparently, Mr. Inside was giving Mr. Outside a few choice parting words. I got the feeling this would be the last time they worked together. "Yeah, yeah, yeah, fuck you."

I didn't wait for "goodbye." A good thing. There wasn't any.

I hit the door full force, rising out of my crouch as I came forward. I might add that my timing was better than the head engineer's at Longines.

I heard him slam down the phone a split second before the door hit his back, like the bang-bang crack of the ball hitting the glove and the foot touching the bag on a close play at first base.

I didn't need one of those instant replays to know that Moses Godley was down and out.

I began screaming like a crazy Mets fan the moment I felt the impact, shouting Nate's name and yelling that there was a gun inside the apartment. The corner of the door hit Godley square in the back, and I used my free left hand to grab hold of his pony tail the instant I burst through the doorway. I was all over him like a closeout suit from Robert Hall. We hit the floor together, but I made sure he took most of the punishment.

There was, of course, one variable that I hadn't fully accounted for in my eleventh hour plan of action.

The gun.

I knew there was a good chance he'd drop it as soon as I lowered the boom. But I didn't know how far it would go. Or in what direction.

Or to whom.

I suppose I was lucky that it landed closest to Cindi West, but then Pablo Johnson wasn't exactly Jesse James himself. She picked it up like a hungry dog pouncing on a bone—quickly but clumsily.

Cindi was standing in the dead center of the room, about four steps from Pablo, who was back against the wall. She turned to hand it to him. He began to step forward to take it. Olympic relay men, they weren't. They were shouting at each other, more frantic than the last time I had seen them together. I seemed to have a negative effect on their relationship.

I took their moment of indecision as an opportunity to crawl for cover behind the nearest available object—one of those giant spool tables that hippies all over were using to spiff up their digs. Godley had covered his with one of those cheap Indian print cloths.

I heard Pablo yell "shoot," then "shoot, I said." Then I heard two shots.

I think she was aiming for me, but there was always the possibility she had decided to fire a couple of practice rounds into the cinder blocks and boards that Godley was using for a bookcase.

The third shot hit a moving target, and so did the fourth.

There wasn't any fifth.

Nate flung the crowbar from the doorway to the next room, and it caught Cindi West right where it counts. She dropped the gun at her feet, then kicked it when she fell to the floor.

The gun landed about eight feet away from me. Pablo went for it. So did I. Nate went for Pablo.

Guess which team won.

Nate picked Johnson up and gave him a bear hug that he wouldn't soon forget. When he was done squeezing, he pushed him to the floor like he was dribbling a basketball. Only Pablo didn't bounce.

"You want a shot at him?" Nate asked.

I sure as hell did, but what was the point? Kicking Pablo Johnson at that moment would have been about as satisfying as French-kissing your little sister.

I walked over to the body slumped against the makeshift bookcase. Moses Godley was breathing, but just barely. One of Cindi's shots had grazed him in the shoulder. The other one had caught him in the chest. He was spilling blood more freely than an old drunk tells his life story. Godley started to tell his, but I told him to save his breath.

"If he buys it, you're up on a murder rap," I said to Cindi.

She was doubled over on her knees, full cycle into a crying jag. It seemed a little late for tears.

"Where's your sister?"

She pointed to the next room. I went into it, then through another doorway to the left.

Sherri West was propped against the wall on a bean bag chair. Her hands were tied—behind her back this time—and there was a gag over her mouth. As usual, she didn't have her clothes on.

"Remember me, the zoo keeper?" I asked.

She nodded. It was hard to tell with the tape over her mouth, but I think she was smiling.

"We'll have you out of here in a few minutes," I told her.

I was taking off my jacket to put over her when Nate joined me in the room.

"You had to get a look, didn't you?" I said.

He shrugged. "A man's got a right to see what all the fuss is about."

It was right about then that Pablo Johnson tried to make one last fuss. He paid for it dearly. He got one foot out the door before I dragged him back inside. I clobbered him once in the midsection, then finished him off with a left to the jaw.

"Dumb idea," I said. "The game's over, Pablo. You lost. You lost big."

Nate went to the window and looked out. "You'd think the cops would have gotten here by now. Four gunshots usually does the trick."

"I'm surprised at your sudden faith in the guardians of the peace. There's a war raging in the park, remember?"

"I know. But Chicago's supposed to be the city that works."

I picked up the phone and called. A woman told me that a car had already been dispatched.

"You better dispatch a couple of ambulances, too," I said. "We've got two injured people here. One of them's about to become a homicide."

I went back into the bedroom and continued untying Sherri West's hands. When I removed the tape from her mouth, she collapsed against me and began to cry furiously. She started trying to talk, and I told her not to strain herself.

Consoling sobbing girls has never been my specialty. Just ask any of the women I've managed to reduce to tears. But I tried my best with Sherri West.

I half carried her into the bathroom and gave her a glass of water. She managed to blurt out "thank you" through strangled sobs. I told her it was nothing, that the worst was finally over. I left her there alone to try to freshen herself up.

When I got back to the living room, I told Cindi to go find her sister something to wear. Then I sat down on the stinking mattress that Moses Godley used for a couch and stared at Pablo Johnson.

I felt nothing but hatred for him and I made sure to let him know it with my eyes. Sitting there with my shirt soaked through with Sherri West's tears, I thought about how I hated everyone who had tried to use this girl to make a buck. The Longs, the Wyders—they were all leeches as far as I was concerned. I didn't stop staring down Johnson until Nate came into the room with two cans of Bud.

"I hope Moses won't mind if we finish off the last of his beer," he said.

"I don't think he's going to mind about much of anything anymore."

CHAPTER **31**

When the cops finally got there, they arrived in force. Naturally, we had some explaining to do. Moses Godley had been shot with my gun, and my prints were all over it.

But contrary to popular belief, some cops are actually willing to listen before they start slapping the cuffs on people and hauling them down to the station. Even when the story they're listening to sounds unbelievable, as ours most certainly did.

It helps if the guy telling the story happens to be one of them. I didn't exactly qualify on that score, but I made some points early on by telling them that I used to be with the New York Police Department. It also helps if you're lucky enough to get a good cop.

We got lucky. His name was Red Kelly. Except for noting that he was about forty-five years old and had my build, I don't need to describe what he looked like. The name says it all.

The first order of business was loading Moses Godley into an ambulance. The paramedics thought his chances were slim to none, but he was still breathing the last time I saw him. Sherri West was feeling well enough to ride to the hospital in one of the police cars with Kelly's partner. Her name could have been Red, too, but it wasn't. She went by Mary O'Brien.

Kelly asked if Sherri had a sister or anything who could meet her at the hospital. I pointed to Cindi.

"I guess she wouldn't be much help, would she?" he said.

I told him about the anything option, and he let me call Marla.

She said she'd leave with Mindi right away, but they had something important to tell us.

"It's about that F. Walker guy," she said. "Mindi knows who he is."

"Are you sure?"

"Positive. Fred Walker. He's a friend of Mr. Long's."

"Arnold or Arnie?" I was getting the high sign from Kelly. Even nice cops lack for patience.

"Arnold. He owns a nightclub. Mindi has a friend who works there as a barmaid. Well, not a barmaid exactly. He's a guy. He's gay."

"Sorry," I said, "I've got to go. But thanks. You have no idea how much help you've been."

Two cops were leading Pablo and Cindi out the door when I got off the phone. Nate couldn't resist the temptation of telling Cindi how cute she looked in handcuffs. Kelly seemed to have a sense of humor, but he didn't appreciate that one.

"I hope you guys don't have any dinner plans," he said. "You're gonna have to come down to the station and answer some questions. A lot of questions."

Oh, yeah. How do you tell a cop you've got an important meeting to go to?

I looked at my watch. It was 2:30. All hell was going to break loose back at Eden if the Bickersons didn't get a call by three o'clock. If I called and told them what was going on, you could be sure someone there would leave and never come back.

"You know about the murder down on Astor Street last night?" I asked Kelly. "A guy named Bill Walters was pushed out his apartment window."

He nodded. "It was a suicide. I heard the guy jumped."

"No, he didn't jump," Nate said. "He was pushed."

"Walters was the PR director for *Nook* magazine," I said. "Before that he was the PR director for *Paradise*."

"That's got something to do with this?" Kelly lit a cigarette. If he did that every time he got impatient, he must have smoked three packs a day.

"It's a long story," I said.

"All your stories are long."

"We can lead you to the person who killed Walters," Nate said. "He's waiting for us—"

"Great. You guys are just swell. A guy knocks somebody off, then he waits around for two detectives to come get him."

"I know it sounds a little strange," I said, "but—"

"It doesn't sound strange. It sounds fucking ridiculous."

"You haven't met the Wyders or the Longs," Nate reminded him.

"Let me get this straight—you're talking about Arnold Long, the guy with all the beautiful broads living down in that Eden estate on Lincoln Park West."

"Yup, that's the guy," I said. "And that's the place we have to get to by three o'clock, or the person who murdered Walters is going to split town."

"It would be a lot easier answering your questions there than down at the station," Nate added. "Have you ever been there?"

Kelly shook his head and lit another cigarette. "I heard all the broads walk around the place without their clothes on. Is that true?"

Nate nodded. "It's a great place," he said. "Mr. Long will probably take you on a tour."

Kelly shook his head again. "Jesus Christ, I don't know. It's probably against regulations."

"But we're leading you to a murderer," I said.

"OK, I guess so. But I gotta take your gun. They're gonna need it for testing down at the lab."

"Sure, whatever you say." I'm a guy who's always willing to compromise when he doesn't have any choice.

As we walked down the rickety stairs, I began to think about what a pair of silver-tongued devils we were.

"One more thing," Kelly said. He was pointing at the suitcase I was carrying in my hand, the suitcase I had picked up off the floor of Moses Godley's bedroom. "What've you got in the bag?"

"Oh, this?" I shrugged. "Just a few odds 'n' ends."

"What kindsa odds 'n' ends."

"Let's see." I peered into the bag. "Couple pairs of underwear, some socks, toothbrush, toothpaste. Two hundred and fifty thousand dollars."

"Gimme that thing," he said. "We're gonna have to take that into evidence, too."

"Better make sure you get a receipt," Nate said.

CHAPTER 32

Having Kelly with us when we entered the gates of Eden was like experiencing the fantasy again for the first time. Kind of like taking your kid to the circus, I would suppose.

His baby blues just about popped out of their sockets when he got a look at the fig leaf desk in the reception area.

"Mr. Long has one in his office that's even bigger," Nate told him.

Kelly shook his head in disbelief, then fixed his gaze on one of the blonde receptionists. By this time, I knew her name was Vicki without having to look at her Paradise name tag. I told her there was no need to fetch anyone, that we were expected. But Arnold Long has his girls well trained. She wiggled her little ass and took off down the hallway ahead of us to warn the boss of our arrival.

"Jesus Christ, how does she walk in that suit?" Kelly asked.

"That's one of the seven joyful mysteries," Nate answered.

By the time we were approaching the Sanctuary, I think Kelly might have been feeling a little disappointed. Thanks in no small part to Nate's inflated images, he had come with fairly high expectations. As yet, he hadn't laid eyes on a single naked girl.

He did get a smile from Vicki, who stopped as she passed us on her way back down the hall. "I just love men in uniforms," she told him.

When she was out of earshot, Nate said, "Don't be shy about

asking her out, Red. These girls give out their phone numbers like you guys hand out parking tickets."

As we entered the Sanctuary for the final time, I got the distinct feeling that the Wyders and Longs didn't share Vicki's fetish about cops. We met with dead silence and hostile stares.

With all the available diversions in the room, you'd think they might have passed the idle time shooting pool, practicing their putting or sitting down for a friendly game of backgammon. But except for Arnold Long, who was busy trying to make himself look busy behind the world's largest desk, the situation was the same as it was when we left.

There was one other exception. This time, I had the feeling we were facing a united front. That would change pretty soon.

The silence only lasted a few seconds before giving way to a chorus of angry demands. Apparently, these folks didn't have any respect for the law. Or at least they weren't intimidated by the presence of a cop. That would change, too.

Nate worked his crowd-control magic by raising his arms and whistling. Then I started with the introductions.

"This is Officer Kelly," I said. "His friends call him Red. I don't think Red would mind if you behave like one of his friends."

Kelly shook his head. He was trying to be attentive, but I could tell he was taking in eyefuls of the scenery every chance he got. It was a natural reaction in that room. As luck would have it, Vicki and one of her associates added to the scenery momentarily when they returned to pour drinks. Red was on duty, of course, so he had to settle for ginger ale.

In an effort to put everyone at ease, Kelly attempted to strike up some small talk with Arnold Long. They teach you that at the police academy. It's where I learned my winning ways.

"I hope you weren't hurt last night," Kelly said.

"Huh? What do you mean?"

"I heard that a policeman hit you during the riot last night. I'm sorry it happened."

"Oh, hell, that wasn't me," Arnold said. "That was Hugh Hefner. They can knock him around whenever they damn well please, as far as I'm concerned."

You had to be in just the right light to see it, but Kelly's face turned red for a moment. I was in the right light.

"Oh, that's right. I'm sorry," he said.

Arnold Long failed to acknowledge the apology.

There seemed to be a unspoken understanding that the free-for-all wouldn't begin until the girls were done pouring drinks. Arnold Long started it off the instant they two-stepped out the doorway. Actually, Len Wyder was faster on the draw, but I deferred to Arnold. After all, it was his booze we were drinking.

"What the hell's going on?" he demanded. "What's *he* doing here?"

Arnold's reference to Kelly was hardly the deluxe tour Nate had promised, but it was plain to see that Red was starting to become more interested in business than pleasure.

"I'm here to investigate a homicide," Kelly said.

"What do you mean? Is one of us under suspicion?"

"If you'll just let me explain, sir—"

"I want my lawyer present," Arnold Long shouted. He turned to Arnie. "Call that kid what's-his-name. Tell him to get his butt down here this minute."

"If he gets to have his lawyer here, I want mine, too," Wyder demanded.

Kelly looked at me and rolled his eyes. "They're not an easy bunch," I said. "You glad you decided to come?"

"It beats working in the park today," he answered. Then he spoke to Wyder. "You want me to read you your rights?"

Wyder motioned at his daughter to pick up the phone. She carried out his orders, just like Arnie did his dad's, only she went about it a little more slowly.

Kelly didn't wait for any motion of counsel before he continued. Watching him reminded me of one of the things I liked about being a cop. You could act like an asshole and get away with it.

"I was called to a storefront apartment on Addison an hour ago to check out a report of a shooting," he said. "There I found Mr. Renzler and Mr. Moore."

"Shooting! Who was it? Not Sherri."

I shook my head. "Sherri's OK, Arnold. We'll get to that."

Long had his hands full trying to keep his mouth shut. He began lighting a cigar to keep himself occupied.

"It was a Caucasian male, approximately fifty years old, named Moses Godley," Kelly said. I glanced around the room for a look of recognition when Kelly pronounced Godley's name. I didn't see any. Whoever was involved in the plot had learned their acting lessons well.

"Or at least that's what he calls himself," Kelly continued. "Renzler and Moore say his real name is Howard. He's in bad shape. We don't think he's going to make it. We took two people into custody—one Caucasian male, approximately thirty years old, named Pablo Johnson. Renzler says his real name is Howard, too. The other was a Caucasian female, about twenty-five, named Cindi West. According to Renzler and Moore, she's the person who pulled the trigger."

The gasps in the room let out enough air to fill up the Goodyear blimp.

"That's right," I said. "Pablo Johnson and Moses Godley plotted with Cindi West to kidnap her sister. Godley is the Reverend Whitey Howard's brother. Pablo Johnson is Whitey's son."

I was sure Kelly didn't understand the significance of those revelations, but he waited for the four of them to catch their breaths before he continued.

"I wanted to take Moore and Renzler down to the station for questioning. But they said they had to meet with you people. They said this case is connected with a murder that took place last night. They said they would explain it all when we got here."

I took another glance around the room. I counted four grim faces. Nate had positioned himself by the door in case anyone tried to make a break for it. With Kelly there, I didn't think that would be necessary.

"By the way," Kelly added. "I had to take your ransom money into evidence. The next time something like this happens, I suggest very strongly that you call the police."

"I *did* call the police," Arnold Long snapped. "They told me it wasn't their jurisdiction."

"Oh."

A young orange-haired fellow strolled into the room while Kelly was busy pulling his foot out of his mouth.

"Who are you?" Arnold Long demanded.

"Mike Murphy, sir. I'm the head of the legal department."

Indeed it was the sole survivor of the purge Arnold had conducted the day Nate and I brought him the bad news about Sherri West. I was impressed with how much time seemed to have passed since then. I was also impressed with the effect a month's success can have on a man.

Murphy had abandoned his department store suit in favor of a three-piece by Christian Dior. He walked straight to the bar and mixed himself a drink, then pulled up a chair beside Arnie and put his feet up on the table. He had taken up smoking a pipe since the last time we met.

"Sorry, Murphy," Long said. Then he motioned at Kelly to continue.

I thought maybe it was time for me to get on with my part of the show, but Len Wyder started peppering the cop with questions before I could begin.

"What's this about a homicide?" he said. "Are you talking about Bill Walters? What does that have to do with any of us? And when do we get our money back?"

"You can ignore him," I advised Kelly. "He's like a minor rash. The kind that won't go away, no matter how much shit you rub on it."

Kelly didn't need any advice. "I know the type," he said.

Wyder was looking at me with hatred in his eyes. The feeling was mutual, I can assure you. He stood up and pointed his finger at me. "As far as I'm concerned, Renzler, you're not workin' for me anymore."

That was worth a laugh, and I didn't bother to stifle it.

Kelly told Wyder to have a seat, then answered one of his questions. "Mr. Renzler and Mr. Moore seem to think someone in this room killed Bill Walters," he said.

There was a hush, followed by a torrent of protest. Arnie Long was the one who protested the loudest.

"What do they know about anything?" He pointed at Nate. "He went and canceled my plane reservations. You went searching through my office, didn't you?"

Nate answered with a shrug and Arnie turned his appeal to Kelly. "You should arrest that man for breaking and entering."

"I didn't break a damn thing, Junior. But yes, I did seach your office. And I found some very interesting things. Plane tickets to Mexico for tomorrow. What a curious coincidence."

I tried to get Nate's attention, but it was no use. It might have been the amphetamines, it might have been thirty hours without sleep, it might have been an intense dislike for Arnie Long. Whatever it was, there was no stopping him until after he had pointed the finger of suspicion right in Arnie's face.

"And one of the plane tickets is for F. Walker," he said. "When I asked you who F. Walker was, you said you never heard of him. Maybe—"

"What?" Arnold Long must have hit just the right frequency to catch Nate's ear. It also helped that he had gotten out of his chair and come all the way around the world's largest desk and out into the middle of the room.

When he started speaking, his comments were directed not at Nate but at his son. I put my hand to my head and groaned. I hadn't gotten a chance to tell Nate about my phone call with Marla.

"Are you going to Mexico with Fred Walker?" Arnold demanded. "You never said anything about that. I talked to Fred just yesterday. He told me he was going out of town on business. What's going on with you two?"

Arnie got up from his chair and stood erect like he was saluting the flag. "Yes, Dad, it's true. I am going away with Fred. And there's something you should know: Fred Walker and I are lovers."

"I don't believe it!" Arnold Long raised his eyes toward the ceiling and yelled as only Arnold Long can yell. "My son! A fucking fruit! With one of my best friends, no less!"

"But Dad! You said I shouldn't have any hangups. You said people should do whatever makes them feel good, as long as they're not hurting anybody. It's the cornerstone of the Paradise ideology. I'm only doing what makes me feel good. I'm only doing what you said I should."

Kelly turned and looked at me. "What the fuck's going on here?" he said.

"Maybe I should explain."

"Yeah. Please do."

CHAPTER **33**

I walked about a third of the way down the room and took a seat on one of the leather-matted surgical tables. It was the same one I had sat on our first day at Eden, the day I learned about body hangup and heard Arnold Long's philosophy of life right from the horse's mouth.

I waited for the father-and-son pissing match to end before I began speaking. It only lasted a few minutes, but I was sure it would continue. Maybe for weeks, maybe for months. After all, they would have years to talk.

"By now, you all pretty much know most of the story behind the kidnapping of Sherri West," I said. "The only thing left for me to do is fill in the blanks. Some of what I'm going to say is conjecture, but most of it—the important stuff at least—is facts."

I paused to light a cigarette. After all the squabbling and interruptions, I finally had their attention. Except for the sound of uneasy shifting in their chairs, there was silence in the room.

"Sherri West was kidnapped with Steve Farrell in Indianapolis by Pablo Johnson and Moses Godley. That part of Bill Walters' story was true. But Walters didn't put up a struggle with them like he said he did, except maybe to take a little bump on the head to make it look good. Because Walters was in on their plan. He wasn't a major player in the game, though. He just lied in return for a cut of the action—was told to lie by someone else who was involved in the plot.

"Steve Farrell was of no use to Pablo and Moses, and Pablo has a sadistic streak in him. So they pumped Farrell full of LSD and dumped him in a cornfield. To write the ransom notes—and the letters that Sherri had been receiving when she was still planning to appear in *Paradise*—Pablo stole stationery from his father, the Reverend Whitey Howard. Why Pablo wrote the threats to Sherri in the first place, we don't really know for sure. But it appears that Sherri had cut him off, and maybe he wanted to get even. But Pablo didn't write the notes himself. He left that task to someone else who wanted to get even with Sherri. Someone who knew what one of Whitey Howard's notes looked like. Someone he had met before Sherri broke things off with him."

"Cindi," I heard Arnold Long murmur from behind a cloud of cigar smoke.

"That's right, Cindi West," I said.

"After Nate paid a visit to Whitey Howard—the day I found Sherri at Steve Farrell's apartment—Pablo's dad began to get a little suspicious. The next time his son came by to see him—the day before yesterday—Whitey probably began pressing Pablo about the notes and the missing stationery. I doubt very much that Pablo liked his father. It might have even been his father who drove Pablo's mother to commit suicide. Pablo took care of his father the same way he had taken care of Steve Farrell."

"Is that the crazy preacher they found down at the corner of Ashland and Madison?" Kelly asked.

"Yup, that's the one," Nate said.

"When the ransom notes arrived, Nate and I became certain that someone inside this group was involved in the kidnapping," I said. "Moses Godley wrote those notes himself. And he made a little mistake. Or maybe it wasn't a mistake. He made reference to a detective in them, which tipped us off that someone from *Nook* or *Paradise* was involved."

"That doesn't mean it's one of us," Arnie said. "What about Walters? He knew we hired you guys. He could have told him."

"Yeah, the kid's right," Len Wyder said. You knew things had come full circle when Wyder was speaking up in support of Arnie Long.

Almost. We weren't quite there yet.

"You're right," I said to both of them. "It could have been Walters. But there was something else that made us suspicious. A few weeks ago, Nate and I went to a restaurant called Steak Your Claim."

"Oh, yeah, I know the place," I heard Kelly mumble.

"On our way out, we saw an unlikely couple dining together." I paused to light another cigarette and watched Boy Wonder and Batgirl exchanging meaningful glances. "Faith? Arnie?"

"We weren't dining together," Arnie Long snorted.

"That's right. I wouldn't eat with him if he had a foot-long cock."

"I was supposed to meet a friend of mine there," Arnie said. "He decided to bring *her* along. He thought we'd have a lot in common."

"That wouldn't have been Fred Walker, would it?" Nate asked. He was beginning to realize just where he had made his mistake.

"Yes, it was Fred," Arnie answered. Despite his recent embarrassment, there was still room for a little righteous indignation in his voice.

"He must've been off in the can when you saw us," Faith said. "Fred had the runs that night."

I resisted the temptation of mentioning what a pleasure that must have been for Arnie.

"Well that explains it then," Arnold Long said. "It was all just a coincidence."

"Oh, yeah, that may have been a coincidence. But it's not all a coincidence, because that's not all of it," I answered. "When Walters found out how much the ransom demand was, he felt like he had gotten screwed. And he had, at least from his standpoint. So he decided to raise his share of the ante by spilling the beans about what he knew." I smiled. "But as we all know, Walters never got a chance to talk. Someone here made sure of that."

"That's preposterous!" Arnold Long sputtered. From my angle, I could see that he was sliding open the top drawer of his desk.

"You better take a peek under the fig leaf, Red. I think he might have a gun in there."

Arnold Long shut the drawer before Kelly got to the desk. No problem. Red opened it again.

"Officer, do you have a search warrant for that?" Mike Murphy was trying to earn his salary.

"Reasonable cause, Junior," Kelly answered. He pulled a small revolver out of the desk. "Saturday night special," he said to me. Then, to Arnold Long: "Do you have a license for this?"

"Yes, I do," Long snapped. "Do you want to see it?"

"Naw, that's OK. I believe you. Besides, you could barely dent a pillow with one of these things. Get yourself an automatic. They're safer."

"After Arnie threw such a snit about giving Walters the money, we began to think maybe he was the one who killed him," I said. "He knew Walters was at home, because Arnold called him. And he ran out of here fast right after the call. That's why Nate searched his office. And when he saw the name F. Walker on one of Arnie's plane tickets and also on Arnie's calendar for the night he was having dinner with Faith—"

"I didn't do it," Arnie yelled. He was standing up and pointing at me. "You're crazy. It was somebody else. What about Pablo Johnson?"

Nate walked over to Arnie and put his hand on his shoulder. "Why don't you sit down and let him finish."

"No, it wasn't Pablo Johnson," I said. "The police report said Walters didn't have any drugs in his system, and that would have been Pablo's method. In addition to that, Walters lived in a high rise. He wouldn't have let Pablo in. He wouldn't have let Arnie in, either."

I pointed at Arnold Long. "Or you." I pointed at Len Wyder. "Or you, either." I paused. "The only person Walters would have let into his building was a woman."

"Not me." It was Faith Wyder's turn to stand up now. Everyone in the room was staring at her.

Before I could respond to her denial, dear old dad took the stand in her defense. "Bullshit! We're not answering any more questions until our lawyer gets here."

"Nobody's asking you any," Kelly said.

Faith was shaking her head. "No, Daddy. There wasn't any answer there when I called."

"What? Whaddaya mean, no answer?"

"While the cat's away, the mice will play," Nate said.

Wyder wheeled and glared at him. I thought for a moment he was going to try something stupid.

"You're not listening, Len." I smiled my charming smile. I have to confess that I was really enjoying making them squirm. It's part of the satisfaction that comes with the job. "I didn't say Faith went to Walters' apartment. I said a woman did."

"Well then, who was it?" Arnold Long sounded a bit impatient.

"After seeing the way Faith handled Arnie in our hotel suite Monday afternoon, Walters would have been afraid to let her in, too," I said. "But he wouldn't have been scared of Cindi West. Walters apparently didn't know Cindi was involved in the plot. After all, he was just incidental hired help.

"Walters was a sucker for money. I'll bet he was a sucker for dames, too. I understand that Cindi worked this turf over pretty good when she used to hang out here. Did she and Walters ever have something going together?"

Arnie Long nodded. The kid was good for something.

"That's what I figured. Walters was just stupid enough not to think things through when she just happened to stop by and ring his doorbell last night."

"You're saying that Cindi West killed Walters?"

"No, Arnold, I'm not. Walters was a cream puff, but you know as well as I do that Cindi couldn't have pushed him out of a window."

"Then it was Pablo Johnson," Wyder said. "Or maybe Godley."

I shook my head. "Johnson was back at Cindi's apartment watching Sherri. I don't know where Godley was, but I don't think he could have gotten all the way down from his place to Walters' apartment in such a short amount of time."

I got up and started walking to the near corner of the room. Faith Wyder was the first one to notice. That made sense. After all, it was her pink suitcase that I was going to get.

"Hey, hey, get away from there." She made a move to come

toward me, but Nate moved faster, grabbing her from behind and pinning back her arms.

I opened the suitcase and reached inside. "There's an envelope full of money here," I said, holding it up for all to see. "If you count it, you'll find two hundred and fifty thousand smackers. What's curious, too, is that none of the bills are marked. I guess Faith decided she'd rather hold on to Arnold's money than her father's."

"Why you goddamn slut bitch." Arnold Long was yelling so loud, his voice carried him right out of his chair.

"That's my daughter you're talkin' about, asshole," Wyder shouted.

"And your daughter's a goddamn slut bitch," Long retorted.

Wyder returned the insult, and suddenly they were all standing and yelling at once. Just like old times.

"Shut up, all of you," Kelly shouted. He didn't have the talent down as well as Nate, but it got the job done. I think it might have helped that he had taken out his gun.

"I didn't do it," Faith yelled. "I kept the money, but I didn't kill anyone."

"I know you didn't," I said. "You stayed behind to give me the money. Only you blew that part, too, because you were off in the powder room when I came to get it. At least that's where the receptionist said you were. She's too dumb to lie for you, or even if she isn't, you wouldn't have trusted her to lie for you."

I looked at Wyder. "You want to tell us about it, Len?"

No he didn't. Not even a little bit.

"I overheard a phone call before we went into Godley's apartment," I said. "You tried to warn him we were coming. At first I thought maybe it was Faith calling, but then I heard him tell you she was an idiot. He said you were an idiot, too—"

Len Wyder picked exactly that moment to confirm Moses Godley's assessment of his mental abilities. Who else but an idiot would think he could pull out a gun and use it when there was a cop standing behind him ready to fire? A Chicago cop, no less.

I was glad that he at least had the sense to turn and aim at Kelly first. At least I think he was aiming at Kelly. There was always the chance he was trying to fire one last shot at Arnold Long, who was standing next to the cop. If he had chosen to shoot at me or Nate, Kelly might not have responded so fast. That's the kind of thing you think about on nights when you can't sleep. That's the kind of thing that gives you sleepless nights.

Wyder never got a chance to fire. One bullet was all it took to kill off Arnold Long's competition.

Nate let go of Faith Wyder's arms, but not before I bent over and picked Daddy's pistol up off the floor. She got down on her knees and leaned over her father and let out a series of ear-splitting, cement-mixer moans.

But she didn't shed any tears.

Neither did Arnold Long. He was too busy continuing his war of words with Wyder. He was shouting—loud, even by his usual standards. It occurred to me that it was a good thing Kelly had taken his gun. If he hadn't, I think Arnold might have used it to kill Wyder a couple of more times.

"You sleazebag! I told you no man would screw Arnold Long and live to tell about it. You're trash, nothing but stinking trash!"

"He can't hear you Arnold," Nate said.

I don't think that made a whole lot of difference to him. He turned to face his son, all the while pointing at the corpse bleeding on his floor. "It's trash like that that gives the entire industry a black eye," he shouted.

"Put a lid on it, Arnold," Nate yelled.

That seemed to do the trick. If it hadn't, Faith Wyder's last hurrah surely would have.

She let out a snarl like a rabid dog and charged across the room like a blitzing linebacker. Like a quarterback blindsided, old Arnold never knew what hit him. She leaped off the floor and hit him feet first—a flying drop kick in wrestling lingo—driving him backward into the world's largest desk. She pinned him against his fig leaf and landed a pair of forearm smashes before Nate and I could intervene. It wasn't easy, but we managed to restrain her while Kelly put on the cuffs.

Arnie went to the phone and called in a plea for first aid. Within moments, the towel blondes arrived to soothe Arnold's ego and nurse him back to health. After a massage and sauna, he'd be ready for that night's party. And somebody from the Paradise Room would surely send over a steak to put on that shiner.

While Kelly called for reinforcements, Nate and I threw the table cloth over Wyder. He may not have been able to steal 250 Gs from Long, but at least he'd get to stick him for a whopper of a laundry bill.

"There's just one thing I don't understand," Nate said. "What did Wyder have to gain from all this? He would have gotten his quarter million back, but what else?"

I shrugged. "A little insurance maybe. A lot of spite."

"Write-offs," a voice behind me said. I turned to see Mike Murphy. In the confusion, I had forgotten he was even in the room. "Not your standard write-offs, of course, but there are ways available to turn a ransom payment into a profit. Or not a profit, but at least a minimization of the loss through a complex series of financial transactions. In fact, that's what Arnie and I have been working on the last few days."

I had a feeling he was about to explain them, but Nate made sure he didn't.

"Sorry I asked," he said to me. Then to Murphy: "I think your client has a great possibility for a civil suit. Why don't you go over there and take a deposition."

"Get lost, you mean," Murphy said.

Nate nodded. "I rest my case."

Just then Kelly's backups started swarming in, and pretty soon Arnold Long's Sanctuary was transformed into a giant rec room for cops. The action today wasn't in the park. It was in that big house across from it where all those beautiful broads walk around without any clothes on.

In Eden.

Unlike Adam and Eve, Nate and I didn't need to be driven out of the place. There was still plenty of unfinished business to attend to—giving statements, getting back my gun, arranging for the return of the ransom money, bidding our final, but not-so-fond, farewells to Arnold and son. But that could all wait for a day.

All of a sudden, I began to feel like a man who hadn't been to sleep for a day and a half. I was so tired, I would have paid a hooker fifty bucks to leave me alone. I didn't feel the need for any company that night, but when Marla stopped by to visit I sure didn't put up any protest.

We stayed in Chicago until Saturday morning, getting out of town just before the final Day of Rage exploded into another riot downtown in the Loop. By that time, I was sitting on my regular barstool back in New York, watching the first game of the World Series on the new color TV at McCabe's.

Mike Cuellar outpitched the Mets' ace, Tom Seaver, and the Orioles won, 4–1. Piece of cake. Three more wins, and I'd be drinking free until New Year's.

Naturally, the regulars all got disgruntled and went home early.

All except one. I stuck around the place licking my chops until closing time.